A RELUCTANT WARRIOR

A RELUCTANT WARRIOR

KELLY BROOKE NICHOLLS

First published in 2017 by The Author People
PO Box 159, St Ives, NSW, 2075 Australia
Copyright © Kelly Brooke Nicholls 2017

National Library of Australia Cataloguing-in-Publication entry

Author:	Nicholls, Kelly Brooke
Title:	A Reluctant Warrior
ISBN:	978-1-925399-20-2 (paperback)
ISBN:	978-1-925399-21-9 (ebook)
Subject:	Thriller
	Political thriller
	Colombia
	Drugs
	Cocaine
	Drug wars
	Colombian cartels
	War on drugs
	Human Rights
Design:	Alissa Dinallo
Cover Photo:	Douglas Frost
Author Photo:	Douglas Frost

Printed by Lightning Source

For Mum and Dad; thanks for all your unwavering support for all my crazy dreams.
And for all the courageous human rights defenders in Colombia and those from abroad who support them.

CHAPTER ONE

Las Delicias, San Juan River, Colombia

A heavyset bulldog of a man, who appeared to be the leader, held in his hands what she knew must be the death list. Whoever was on that list would be killed, and these animals liked to make their victims suffer. He smiled as he looked around the football field. The people of Las Delicias huddled together. They were surrounded by more than thirty men in jungle fatigues, machetes strapped to their backs, carrying assault rifles. Luzma put her arm protectively around her younger brother, Jair, and glanced at her grandparents who stood beside them. Would she and her family be on that list?

There had been signs that this was coming. Rumors had traveled downriver of a paramilitary takeover of the area. A week ago a dismembered body had washed ashore. People had begun to flee. But many refused to leave. This land was all they had, all they had ever known.

'Good afternoon, Las Delicias,' the leader said. 'We are the Black Eagles.'

Luzma stared at the men before her. A similar paramilitary group had taken her mother ten years earlier. Some of the same men may have been involved.

'We are fighting the guerrilla scum destroying our beautiful country. The only way Colombia can be great again is if we kill every last one of those parasites and all of their friends. If you are an ally of the guerrilla or if you have helped them in any way, you are our enemy.'

Luzma felt her face flush with anger. Nobody in Las Delicias had helped the guerrilla. The people here were simple farmers and fishermen, not part of this godforsaken war.

The leader held up the list again, scanning the crowd. 'We want the following people: Roberto Gonzalez, Enrique Pena, Federico Rojas, Manuel Martinez.' The sound of wailing women and sobbing men drowned out his voice, causing him to pause.

Luzma's heart broke seeing Manuel, her friend, being dragged away by two of the paramilitaries. His mother clung to his hand, refusing to let go despite being kicked and punched by the men. Old Dona Rojas fell to her knees, pleading for her husband to be let go.

'Where are you taking my Papa?' Doctor Pena's son cried, running after his father.

She had to stop this. These people were innocent. They were friends, neighbors.

'These people have done nothing wrong,' Luzma said. Silence settled as everyone stared at her. Luzma swallowed the lump that had formed in her throat. 'If these people gave the guerrilla food or shelter when they were here, it is because a gun was held to their heads. They have nothing to do with this stupid conflict. All we want is to be left in peace.'

'What would your name be, princess?' the bulldog asked as he walked towards her.

'Luz-Marina Cuesta.' She stepped in front of Jair and felt her grandparents flanking her on either side.

The leader stood so close that she could smell the rum and tobacco on his breath. He turned to his men and said with a lecherous smile,

'Well, boys, I think Las Delicias is going to be delicious.'

Luzma felt naked in her little shorts and singlet top as the men's eyes moved over her. It was that sickly feeling of vulnerability she knew all too well. She clenched her hands at her sides to stop them from shaking. She would not let them see her fear.

'These people have done nothing wrong,' she repeated slowly, hoping they couldn't hear the tremble in her voice. 'There is no-one in this community who has supported the guerrilla.'

'Mmm, I love little troublemakers like you; it's so sexy. Boys,' the bulldog said, turning to his men, 'we're going to have a wild one tonight.'

The men jeered, making lewd gestures.

'José,' he said, addressing one of his men, 'take my new girlfriend and her family back to their house and make sure they don't leave. I want her well rested for tonight.'

CHAPTER TWO

The paramilitary officer guarding them burst through the front door.

'Give me a drink. I'm thirsty.'

'What would you like?' Grandpa asked.

The man walked straight across to Luzma. 'What's that aphrodisiac you all drink in Choco? I hear it keeps you very hot.'

Luzma stared at him defiantly.

'I'm speaking to you.'

Scenes from ten years ago flashed through her mind, sending a chill down her spine.

'You mean *borojoa* juice?' Grandma said, moving towards him.

'Yes, bring me one of those, gorgeous.' He winked at Luzma and returned to the balcony.

Luzma exhaled slowly. She had to do something before the other soldiers arrived. She had to escape, as she knew all too well what would happen to her and her family.

'Grandma do we still have the *dormilona* mixture?' Luzma whispered.

Her grandmother looked at her a long moment, the lines around her weathered forehead deepening. She went to her special cupboard and pulled out dried herbs and little jars of liquids. Her 'magic potions' Jair called them. She was famous as the best *curandera* in the area and Luzma was her trainee. People from all over River San Juan would travel to Las Delicias so she could heal them with her herbs.

'Are you going to poison him?' Grandpa asked, his eyes darting between Luzma and the door.

'He asked for a drink. I'm going to give him a special one. He'll be fast asleep in no time.'

Luzma helped her grandmother mix ground herbs of the *garde* and *dormilona* plants and clear liquid together with juice of the *borojoa* fruit. They were the same herbs they had mixed up for a client who had come to see them several weeks ago with severe insomnia. The man had been at the point of insanity and had insisted on trying the potion straightaway in their living room. It had only taken him five minutes and he'd been fast asleep on the sofa, the first time he'd slept properly in months.

'I can go with you,' Jair said, his big eyes looking up at Luzma.

'No, it's best I go alone.' She walked to the door.

The man was fidgeting with his assault rifle and as Luzma stepped onto the balcony he swung around and aimed the rifle at her chest. She almost let the glass slip from her hand. There was a deadly silence broken only by her sharp, shallow breaths. She stood, staring at the dark grey muzzle of the rifle that was only an a few centimeters away.

'Can I have my drink?'

She handed him the glass and the bottle of rum, her hands shaking.

He took a swig of the rum and then stared at the purple juice.

'So this is the famous *borojoa* drink.' He brought the glass to his lips, studying her intently. 'Why are you so nervous, princess?'

'The gun makes me nervous,' she said, forcing away the images from the past.

He drew the point of the gun away from her chest, moving it up the inside of her thigh, all the way up. 'Would you like some rum to loosen you up for tonight?'

She resisted the urge to spit on him, remaining silent instead.

He smiled as he looked up the road. The sun was sinking into the jungle, throwing long shadows over the town. 'They'll be coming soon. Maybe I should have my drink.' He took the glass, watching her as he drank it all and then slowly licked his lips.

'So, princess, do you have a boyfriend?'

She ignored him, waiting for the drink to take effect.

'Don't worry, princess, you'll have lots of boyfriends tonight,' he said, slurring his words. 'Mmm, this rum has a kick to it. Are you sure you don't want some?' He shook his head, as if trying to rid himself of whatever was taking over his body. He slumped against the wall.

The music from the football field stopped.

He grinned. 'It seems the party is moving down here.' His body sagged and his eyes closed.

She gingerly shook his arm. It was limp. She stood staring at him for a moment before the door opened and Grandpa came out.

'Let's go,' she said. 'We have to make it to the jungle before they get here.'

The men up the hill were laughing and shouting, their voices moving closer. Luzma grabbed Jair's hand and ran down the side of the house. She peered around the corner. The paramilitaries were stumbling down the hill, rum in hand, dragging some women with them.

'Keep low and hide in the shadows,' Luzma whispered to her grandparents who were crouched behind her.

'Don't wait, Luzma,' Grandma said. 'Whatever happens, you and Jair just keep on going.'

The thought of the bulldog's eyes propelled her forward and she ran, crouching to keep out of sight.

Luzma's heart pounded. The jungle was about 100 meters away but the area in front of them was exposed. The paramilitaries would be at the house any second and would find the unconscious guard. They would hunt them down. Luzma sprinted, dragging Jair's tiny body along with her.

They reached the jungle's edge, stopping for just a moment to see if their grandparents were behind them.

'Don't stop and don't look back,' Luzma said, taking the lead. The jungle was her sanctuary where she had spent hours every week exploring.

'I'll stay at the back and will distract them if they catch up to us,' Grandma said, panting.

And then they were off, running through the thick maze of foliage. Behind them, an eruption of angry voices.

Luzma went faster, dragging Jair behind her. Exposed branches and prickly plants slashed at her naked legs. A stump caught her feet. She lurched forward, grabbing a tree to regain her balance. She couldn't stop.

'Find that bitch!' the leader screamed from somewhere behind her.

God, please help us escape.

Her legs and chest were burning, but she could not stop. She would prefer to be killed than captured. She ran and ran, leaving Las Delicias behind as a memory.

'No more,' Grandma said between heaving breaths. 'I can't run any further.'

Luzma could just make out her grandma in the darkness that was enveloping them. She sounded as if she was drowning, desperately gasping for air. How had she managed to get this far? They had run for what felt like hours, too afraid to stop. They were now between Las Delicias and the next community, Pereas.

Luzma fanned her grandmother and gently rubbed her back.

'We can't go to Pereas as they'll probably send people there to look for us,' Luzma said. 'Grandpa, do you think your friend Luis Jorge would help us?'

Luis Jorge was an eccentric old fisherman who lived by himself in a cabin between the two communities. He had a motorized canoe that he used to travel upriver to sell his fish.

'I'm sure he will,' Grandpa replied.

'What if the paramilitaries go to Luis Jorge's place as well?' Jair asked, still gripping Luzma's hand.

'Let's hope they don't.'

'Let's go,' Luis Jorge said. 'We don't have long before the sun comes up and makes this more difficult.'

He set off into the jungle, his long legs moving briskly. They walked in silence, struggling to make out the path ahead of them in the near total darkness. The sounds of the jungle were magnified; the rustling of animals moving through the bushes, the owl's whistle, the melancholy song of the Guaco bird and a myriad of other mysterious noises.

They walked down the valley into the mangroves, wading through the muddy water. Luis Jorge turned on his flashlight, revealing the motorized canoe tied to the mangroves alongside a narrow tributary. As they got in, the water rose up, almost spilling into the canoe. The chances of a quick escape if they ran into the paramilitaries were slim.

Grandpa and Luis Jorge paddled so as not to draw attention with the sound of the engine. Luzma wrapped her arms around Jair and tried to avoid the branches that jutted out across the narrow waterway. It would take hours to get to San Juan River, according to Luis Jorge. But he probably wasn't the only one to know these waterways. Both the guerrilla and the paramilitaries used them to move coca leaves to their jungle laboratories and to transport the goods out to the Pacific Ocean. Hopefully they would not come this way tonight.

As they emerged from the jungle into the main river, the skies burst and rain cascaded down like a waterfall. The sun was rising on the horizon. Luzma had no idea what the day would bring. She had been so focused on escaping that it was only now that she thought about what they had left behind, the community where she'd spent the past ten years of her life and her friends, the only people outside her family she could trust. Remembering those screams she had heard from the football field, she did not even know if her friends were alive.

Jair was obviously thinking the same thing, asking, 'When can we go back home?'

'I'm not sure,' Grandma replied.

It was the first time Luzma had ever heard her grandmother without an answer. Tears formed, merging with the pelting rain. She watched the water as it rushed past the canoe, taking them further and further into the unknown.

Her life would never be the same – of that she was certain.

CHAPTER THREE

Buenaventura, Colombia

'When will I receive the five million dollars?' General Ordonez asked.

'Patience, General.' Pablo Ruiz lit his cigar and exhaled slowly. 'I will have it to you in the next week or two.'

Ruiz would have liked to swindle the greedy bastard out of his money. But he needed him. This was the most audacious plan he had ever come up with and even he could not do it without the General on his side.

'We helped you take over barrio San Francisco more than three months ago as agreed. You have uninterrupted access to the factory but still I have not received the majority of my money,' the General's voice rose as he spoke. 'You have until the end of the week or the deal is off.'

Pablo knew the factory was critical. This wasn't a little project he could put together in the jungle. The factory had been used in the past to build large-scale fishing vessels, so it had the space and moving equipment he needed.

'Relax. I will get you the money,' Pablo said.

The General's gaze was intense, his body rigid. 'I don't think you understand. My career is at risk. If I am discovered helping you with this plan I will not only lose my job, I will probably be extradited to the US on drug charges. I want my money now and I want you to get this moving. I can't keep it quiet for too much longer.'

Pablo exhaled a puff of smoke. 'Don't talk to me about risks. If this doesn't work out I'll be killed.' Not to mention his children. Pablo remembered the meeting he had had with his boss, the head of the Norte de Valle cartel, after the interception of his shipment of one thousand kilos of cocaine to the US hidden in the hollowed out legs of massive, rustic tables. Fernando Guitterrez, or El Magico as he was widely known, had put photos of his two children on the table.

'Fabricio and Nelly are their names I believe,' he said, looking at Pablo.

Pablo felt cold all of a sudden. He didn't care about anyone in the world apart from his children.

'Yes,' he said, trying to calm his voice.

Fernando took his time. 'You must love them very much.'

'I do,' Pablo said through gritted teeth.

'Make sure this plan of yours works. I will give you the amount of money you're asking for. But you need to understand. If this doesn't work I will take both of your children and torture them — in front of you. They will die a slow, painful death and they will know it was their father's fault. Do you understand?'

Pablo nodded. He had no choice.

'I will have my money by Friday?' The General asked, bringing Pablo back to reality.

'Yes.'

'I want you out of the factory in a month. The human rights groups are protesting loudly after the takeover. I can't risk any more national or international attention.'

'I'm not sure we can move it that quickly.'

'Find a way.'

CHAPTER FOUR

As soon as they paddled around the final curve of the river, they were confronted by the sight of ships the size of five football fields queued up as far as they could see in the port of Buenaventura. The wash from one of the tankers being pulled into position by a tugboat suddenly swamped their tiny canoe and it came dangerously close to capsizing.

Buenaventura's harbor buzzed with production. Endless rows of cargo containers were stacked on top of one another like dominoes. A yellow crane pulled one from the pile, trying not to let them all fall to the ground.

'Welcome to Buenaventura, Colombia's principal port city,' Luis Jorge said, pulling the canoe alongside a crowded wharf.

In contrast to the silence of their trip down river, this city seemed to operate with a constant cicada-like chatter.

'*Minutos a todos los operadores, Comcel, Movistar,*' one man shouted, selling mobile phone minutes.

'*Chondaduro, banano, mango, guanabana,*' another one said, peddling fruit.

'*Jaiba, cangrego, calamar, tilapia, camarones, piangua, lisa, pelada, pargo rojo, bocachico,*' a man bellowed the full listing of seafood he had on offer.

'Thank you so much, *hermano,*' Grandpa said to Luis Jorge. 'We owe you our lives.'

'When do you think you'll be back?'

'Whenever they leave for good. Who knows when that will be.'

It suddenly hit Luzma that they had no home, no community, no friends, no money, no food. There was no going back, for now. She stepped onto the wharf. Jair scrambled up beside her, grabbing her hand tightly.

'What are we going to do here?' Jair asked, looking up at her.

'We'll call Auntie Jolene and she'll help us,' she said. 'Don't worry. We'll be safe here.'

Luzma had rarely seen any hesitation or doubt on her grandfather's face. He had always been composed, in control of every situation. Even when her mother was taken she couldn't remember seeing him cry. He just disappeared to the mountains and then returned to do what was needed. Today, however, a flicker of hesitation wrinkled his face as he climbed onto the wharf.

Grandma went to one of the men on the wharf who provided mobile phones and called her sister, Jolene.

'She's coming to get us,' she said, smiling as she returned.

'Hermanita!' Grandma cried, hugging her sister.

Jolene's face was overtaken by an enormous semi-toothless smile. She was older than her sister and grey curly hair escaped from under her African-print headscarf.

'Luzma, look at you!' Jolene said, hugging her so hard she could barely breathe. 'You've grown into such a beautiful woman,'

'Ah and this *flaco*, you got your Grandpa's skinny genes!' she said, swallowing up Jair in a bear hug. 'You all look like drowned rats. I suppose you didn't have time to bring anything with you.'

Jolene knew what it was like to run for her life. Luzma had heard the stories of how her great aunt used to live in Tumaco, farther south on the Pacific Coast, where she was a community leader but was threatened by the guerrillas so she and her family fled to Buenaventura.

'Come on, let's get you to our place,' she said, leading them to the road. 'Between the kids and the neighbors we'll find you some new clothes.'

The center bustled with people, taxis and motorbikes. There were policemen and soldiers on nearly every corner and they looked ready for battle, weighed down by full army fatigue, flak jackets, helmets and assault rifles.

'Jolene, why are there so many soldiers here?' Is there's a w-w-war here as well?' asked Jair.

Jolene smiled, patting him on the back. 'No need to worry, my dear. It's just that this is a very important city. It's where nearly all the goods enter and leave and right now we're in the heart of it, right near the port, but also the local government offices,' she said, pointing to the enormous building to their right. 'The army is just making sure there are no problems.'

Her voice was barely audible above the music from a corner café bar. People sat around drinking and shouting at each other over the top of the pounding salsa music. The songs were familiar to Luzma, but the setting was in stark contrast to the home she had left behind.

They walked away from the harbor to an area crowded with mini-vans and taxis competing for clientele. Jolene led them to a bus that was about to leave. Luzma's head bumped against the window as the mini-bus impatiently jerked in and out of the traffic. There was a cacophony of sounds, horns contending for air space, and a seeming surround sound of different music, salsa from the car beside them, *vallanato* from the clothes shop on the corner and *regatton* from the bar on the other side. Jair held onto her arm as if she was his safety blanket and peered cautiously out the window.

'There are so many cars here,' he said.

Nobody had cars in Las Delicias. The river and the waterways were their roads. Unlike Luzma, who had spent her time traveling around the region searching for her mother and helping other people who had lost family members do the same, Jair had barely left Las Delicias.

'This is the entrance to San Francisco,' Jolene said as the bus turned right, down a small side road.

Houses crowded either side of the street, paint peeling and corrugated iron roofs rusted to the red-brown color of the football field in Las Delicias. Bunches of ripe bananas hung out the front of one house and beside it was a small barber. As they traveled down the road things began to change. The bus bumped on the gravel road and the brick homes were soon replaced by old grey timber beams slapped together, with black plastic covering the holes and acting as a roof in some cases.

The bus stopped abruptly.

Jolene eased herself out of the seat and motioned them forward.

'This is as far as the bus will go.'

Outside a group of teenage boys scrutinized everyone who got off the bus. They whistled as Luzma stepped out and before she was able to stop him, one pinched her bottom. Without thinking she swung around and slapped him, leaving the side of his face red.

Jolene grabbed her hand and pulled her away, leaving the boy swearing after her.

'Luzma,' Jolene hissed. 'You must be careful. Things have changed a lot here in the past couple of months. You could get yourself into a world of trouble doing something like that. You're not in Las Delicias anymore.'

That much was obvious. Luzma covered her nose; the smell of raw sewage was overwhelming.

'Many people who live here have been displaced from other areas,' Jolene whispered. 'The government doesn't provide them with any help so they make their own homes. Sadly, there is no running water or sewerage system.'

A mangy dog covered in flies sniffed at them. Plastic bottles that were strewn on the ground crackled under their feet. Jair walked a beat behind her, trying to hide in her shadow. Laughter lightened the air and Luzma looked up. A group of kids raced old tires down the road. From the direction they were running was an empty field with short shrubs and a few palm trees. Far in the distance were two enormous adjoining buildings, both about the size of a football field and at least two stories high. They sat at the junction of two rivers.

'What are those?' Luzma asked, pointing to the two buildings.

'Those factories used to store all the timber that came in from around the Pacific and many years ago industrial fishing boats were built there. But, now,' Jolene glanced around. 'They're off limits. You mustn't go near them.'

'Why?' Luzma asked.

'You've just arrived. I'll tell you about them some other time.'

Jolene's house was down a small dusty road. It stood on stilts over muddy water full of garbage. There were some holes in the walls where the builders had run out of wood. The house had two small bedrooms, one for Jolene and her husband, Lucho, and the other for her daughter Estella who lived there with her five-year-old daughter, Liliana. The other children had moved out or away from Buenaventura. A cross, candles and Orisha beads sat in a little altar in the tiny living room. The kitchen was at the back and the toilet was on an uncovered balcony above the smelly water, with a rudimentary curtain around it.

'I don't have much to offer, but everything I do have is yours. We'll set up a bed for you all to share in the living room and we'll get you a good lunch. I'm sure you're starving.'

'Ah, *hermanita, mil gracias*,' Grandma said, tears running down her face as she embraced her sister again.

Lucho came in to greet them. He was a tall, sinewy man with the same quiet reserve as Grandpa. He was also a fisherman by trade and offered to show Grandpa and Jair around the waterfront and to get a fish for lunch.

After they'd settled in, Grandma, Jolene and Luzma set about preparing lunch as if the routine would make them feel more at home.

'You know we're so incredibly lucky, Luzma,' Grandma said, grating coconut.

Luzma was happy the onion she was cutting gave her an excuse for her watery eyes. She couldn't stop imagining what had

16

happened to all their friends in Las Delicias. She had to be strong for her family.

Grandma squeezed the juice out of the grated coconut, the off-white liquid trickling through her hands.

'When our ancestors were taken from their land in Africa and hauled across the Atlantic in the most appalling conditions, they arrived in a land so foreign to them that they didn't even know the language. They missed their homes just like we do.' Her grandmother paused, throwing the onion, tomato and garlic into the frying pan, oil spitting.

'They didn't have family to greet them like we do,' she said, smiling at Jolene who was frying pieces of *platano* in a pool of the sizzling oil. 'They were met by these strange unwelcoming people who would become their masters and who would control every hour of their day.'

CHAPTER FIVE

The bulldog put a knife to Luzma's throat and the other men encircled her as their eyes grazed her body. She struggled to escape. They closed in on her. Then suddenly she was fifteen again. The paramilitary officer laughed as he left her crumpled on the floor, pulling her stained white dress over her.

She wrenched herself from the depths of the nightmare. The same one she'd had every single night since she had arrived at Aunt Jolene's house. She was damp with sweat.

Grandma, Grandpa and Jair were still asleep on the floor beside her. Jolene's living room had become their home since they escaped Las Delicias two weeks ago. But she had nothing. So they all slept together on the prickly wooden floor with just a blanket and a single sheet that they wrestled with in their sleep.

But they were the lucky ones; they'd escaped after all. Luzma's mind was plagued by those screams she had heard.

She sat up and looked at her family's bodies curled around each other beside her. Her Grandma and Grandpa's faces were haggard and tired. Luzma knew it must be so difficult to start again and rebuild a new life, in a new city. It made her more determined to try harder to earn money to ease the worry and burden.

The makeshift plastic door flapped open in the wind. It was the only thing blocking the kitchen from the outside toilet and sewage-laden mud below.

Luzma passed her grandfather a cup of *agua con panela*.

'Don't worry, Grandpa,' Luzma said, forcing a smile. 'I'm going to find some work today. I'm sure of it.'

'I'm going to find some work as well, Grandpa,' Jair said.

'What exactly are you going to do, *Flaco?*' Luzma laughed. 'Twelve-year-old boys can't work!'

'I can make money as well,' Jair said, puffing out his tiny chest and pursing his lips.

'Luzma, we have two people who need our help this morning. Do you mind if you go by yourself to one?' Grandma asked, as she entered the room.

'It's a young woman Jolene has helped a lot since she arrived in Buenaventura five years ago. Her daughter is sick and the doctors haven't been able to help.'

'Of course.'

'Are any of these people paying?' Grandpa asked.

Grandma shot him a stern look. She stepped closer, hands on her hips, dwarfing him with her rotund body.

'You know very well, *Teofilo*, that it is not us who heals but the spirits, so we can't ask for money.'

Luzma had heard the same message repeated constantly. They were blessed with the ability to hear the spirits' wisdom and use it to help people. It was a gift and knowledge that had been brought with their ancestors from Africa and passed down through their family. They couldn't profit from it.

'I know, my love,' Grandpa said quietly. 'We need the money to survive, and you and Luzma have already managed to get quite a clientele.'

It had not taken long for people to learn about Grandma's skills as a *curendera*. Already the sick had begun appearing at Joelene's door, a flicker of hope in their eyes, carrying their illnesses and ailments like a heavy weight they were ready to offload. Grandma never rejected anyone for it would be going against the spirits' wishes to do so, nor did she ever ask for anything in return. Luzma was her trainee and ever since she was a child, she had the ability to feel another's pain and find the source. After her mother was taken ten years ago, she and Jair had moved to Las Delicias and she had started to work with her grandmother to learn the many natural remedies she used. At least in that way she could help people.

'I'll go see the girl this morning and then I'll ask in all the shops and restaurants if they have any work. I'm sure there will be an opening.' She hoped she could find paid work, as she didn't know how long her family could continue to live off Jolene's meager wage.

A man dressed in army fatigues sat on an old sofa with a young girl on his lap. The child, who had the same long black hair and delicate bone structure as her mother, Diana, was crying. The man rubbed her back gently and whispered to her.

'This is Mauricio,' Diana said, pointing to the young soldier who was now rocking the girl in his arms. 'And this is my daughter, Valentina. I don't know what happened to her, but for the past two months she has been fading away. She refuses to eat and she barely talks and all she does is cry. I don't know what to do.'

'Did something happen at the time this started?'

'No. She is always with me or Mauricio or at school. I've asked her teachers and they can't explain it either.'

Luzma crouched before the girl and spoke to her softly but received no response. The girl's skin was cold and dry, despite the warm air. Her stomach was extremely bloated and her pulse was soft and hard to detect; it was as if she was indeed slipping away. Her eyes were sunken and glazed. Luzma had seen that kind of look before.

'Did the doctor do tests on her?' she asked, although she already knew in her gut that what this girl had would not be found in any doctor's examination.

'They did all sorts of tests. I went back several times until they finally said that nothing was wrong with her and it must just be depression that had stopped her eating and led to the other symptoms. But why would a five year old be depressed?'

'Is there any reason that someone would want to hurt you?' Luzma asked. 'It seems to me that she has *mal de ojo*, where a bad spirit has taken over her.'

'You mean someone has put a spell over her?' the woman asked, her fine forehead furrowed.

'I know it can sound a little strange if you haven't heard it before, but I have seen it many times and Grandma has many stories about young children being affected by what she calls the evil eye. Sometimes people simply carry evil spirits and because children are so innocent and susceptible they can get them just by looking at that person. Other times people purposely put spells over children to get to their parents due to jealousy or hatred. So you need to ask yourself, is there anyone who might bear a grudge against you?'

'Maybe religious zealots who don't approve of my profession, or one of the other girls who is jealous because I get more clients than they do, perhaps a wife whose husband uses my services or one of the men who wants to own me and can't handle that they are nothing more than money to me. I probably have many enemies,' the woman said nonchalantly.

Luzma stared at the stunning young woman before her and then to the young army officer, whom she assumed was the woman's boyfriend. He was combing the child's hair and didn't seem to care about what Diana was revealing; but she couldn't have been more than twenty-five.

'In that case I'm pretty sure that your daughter has *mal de ojo*. She has all the symptoms and it's something that a traditional doctor can never test for.'

'What can I do for her?' Diana asked.

'It's not too hard to treat. We need to get you the herb *celedonia* and from that we can make a liquid which she will take several times a day until her malaise goes away.'

'That's it? Are you sure she will get better?'

'I'm sure. We treat these cases a lot.' Luzma smiled at her gently. 'I'll make it up for you this afternoon. Can you pick it up from Jolene's house tonight?'

'Definitely,' Diana said, scooping her daughter up into her arms. 'Thank you so much. If this works I will always be indebted to you.'

'When this works you have the spirits to thank, not me.'

'This is my phone number. If you ever need help call me, I know everyone here,' she said, handing Luzma a piece of paper. 'Buenaventura is a dangerous city for everyone, especially for young women. The innocent and naïve don't survive too long here.'

CHAPTER SIX

Luzma left the house tangled up in her thoughts. So much so that she lost track of time and when she looked up she had no idea where she was. There were two boys about Jair's age playing soccer in the street.

'Which way to the center?' she called out to them.

One of the boys pointed diagonally in front, so she rounded the corner and was blinded by the sun. She covered her face to see where she was going. A group of young men sat on the next corner playing dominoes. Their gazes weren't on the game; they were on her. She stopped and looked around. She could turn back from where she'd come but that street was empty apart from the boys. At least in front there were other people around and not just these men. She stared intently at the road and walked briskly. Her skin crawled as their shadows stretched across the road as she passed them.

'So, cutie, what's your name?' one of them asked, stepping in front of her. He wore his cap backwards and his jeans loose.

'Luz-Marina.' She tried to sound casual.

'And where do you live?' a tall muscular man with a shaved head asked.

'San Francisco,' she said, glancing around inconspicuously to see where the other people on the street had gone.

The man with the baggy jeans stepped closer to her, the rum on his breath washing over her. The smell reminded her of the paramilitary officer from ten years ago. The man took her chin and tilted her face up to his.

'You're very pretty,' he said. 'Maybe you'll have to be my girlfriend.'

'I have better taste than that,' she said, pushing his hand away from her face.

'What did you say?' he asked, his tone menacing.

'Leave her alone,' a deep voice with a thick accent called out.

The men stepped back revealing a tall man with broad shoulders and honey-colored skin. He walked towards them, his green eyes locked on the man who had been talking to her.

'She's obviously new to town. She doesn't know anyone. Let her go.' He stopped meters in front of the three men.

They stepped towards him, jaws jutting out, chests puffed. He held his ground, his gaze didn't shift.

'Who are you?' one of them asked.

'You know who I am. Rafael Wilson. I work for Peace Brigades International,' he said, pointing to the insignia on his cream jacket. 'Look, I'm taking the girl with me.' He gestured for her to go with him.

She stood still, looking between him and the men.

'This is our neighbourhood,' one of the men said, exaggerating each word. 'We set the rules.'

'That's fine, you can keep the neighborhood. But the girl isn't from here and she doesn't want to stay.' He sidestepped the bald man and held out his hand to her. 'Shall we get out of here?'

She stared at him. Who was this foreigner? Could she trust him? She decided she would prefer to take her chances with him rather than stay with these men. She took his hand. It was warm and his grip firm. He pulled her forward and they started to walk away. Her harassers whispered amongst themselves. The foreigner strode away, taking her with him.

'If either of you come back here again you'll be in trouble,' one of the men called after them.

24

'I'm from the US,' Rafa said, leaning back in his chair. 'I've been here for three years now. I intended to be here for just a year on a research grant, but then I fell in love and couldn't leave.'

A touch of disappointment tugged at Luzma, she had enjoyed the handsome foreigner's attention and his keen interest in her work as a healer. But she quickly dismissed the feeling. She forced an awkward smile. 'Well, they say love makes you do crazy things.'

'No, I don't mean I fell in love with a woman,' he said with a laugh. 'I fell in love with Buenaventura, with the people. A human rights activist who made a big difference in my life ten years ago when I was in a really dark place taught me about the Afro-Colombian struggle. From then on I always wanted to be involved and help in some way.'

The restaurant was in the style of a massive cabana with wide open windows overlooking the bay. Small artisan fishing boats bobbed in the shimmering water and a man paddled a canoe laden with the day's catch.

'Look at this place: I love the ocean, the rivers, the mangroves, the food, the music.'

His passion was contagious. Buenaventura appeared more beautiful than Luzma had previously noticed. She took a bite of her fish stew and inhaled the smells of coconut, lime and cilantro.

'You mentioned that you work for Peace Brigades International. What exactly is that?'

'It's an international organization that works with local human rights defenders who are under threat. We provide physical accompaniment but also get our allies in the US and European governments to put added pressure on the national and local government in order to offer greater protection.'

'Does it actually work?' she asked and then realised how rude she must sound. 'I mean, from my experience, the paramilitary and the guerrilla do whatever they want. They're the ones who are armed after all.'

'You're right, but they still care about their image and international presence and the pressure makes them think twice.'

She wondered if that would have made any difference to her mum. She doubted it. The real reason she was taken was not her work as a human rights defender, but because she confronted the paramilitary leader on what one of his officers had done to Luzma.

'What's the situation here? Who are you protecting?' she asked.

He looked at her intently. 'No-one has told you about Buenaventura, have they?'

'Not exactly. I've never been here before and my great aunt hasn't told us a lot. I think she doesn't want to stress my family anymore at this stage. But I'm not stupid. She says we can't go near the factory, we can't go out at night by ourselves and I have to be polite to the young men that seem to patrol the streets. Obviously the paramilitaries and guerrilla here are like everywhere else in this country.'

'You've seen a lot of them in your life?' he asked.

'You could say that,' she said simply, not knowing how much she could trust him. She hadn't explained in any detail why she and her family had come to Buenaventura, just that they were new.

'Well, I don't want to scare you but I think for your own safety it's best you know the real situation.' He paused, his gaze soft. 'You're a very attractive young woman and as you saw today, they pick on people like you.'

'Who were they?'

'This whole city is controlled by the army, the paramilitaries or the guerrilla. Like you said, the same as the rest of the country, but just more intense and more concentrated. The area where we were today, known as the Bajarmar, is fought over by the paramilitaries and the guerrilla. Each barrio is controlled by one group and there are streets, like the one you crossed today, that border those barrios.'

Luzma shook her head. 'I wish I could find a place they hadn't gotten to, somewhere that would be safe for my family and me. Does that even exist?'

'I'm not sure,' Rafa said with a shrug.

'So what about San Francisco? That's where we're staying with my great aunt.'

'That's an interesting story,' Rafa said, pausing to take a sip of his *lulo* juice. 'It was controlled by the guerrilla up until recently. Then about three months ago the number of deaths and forced disappearances went through the roof. The paramilitary, with the army's help, took out all the guerrilla leaders and gave their men the option: join them or be killed.'

Luzma's felt cold, despite the early afternoon sun on her skin.

'What was the reason to take over the neighbourhood, or did they do it just for the hell of it?'

'No-one knows. But it has something to do with the factory on the outskirts of the barrio. The owner and his son were killed and the rest of the family have fled. Now no-one can get near there.'

'What are they doing in the factory?' Luzma asked.

'No idea.'

'You said the military is involved as well,' she said.

Rafa began to twist the silver ring on his thumb.

'Some of the soldiers and the police officers are really good people who just want to help to make this place safer. But others, including the leaders of the local army division, are corrupt, have an intense hatred for the guerrilla or a desire to gain a promotion or a trip based on their "body count". Whatever their reason, the reality is, that in many circumstances, they collaborate with the paramilitaries and some even commit atrocious human rights abuses themselves.'

'Like what?'

He looked around. The table beside them was empty but behind a group of men in business suits were finishing their lunch. A few tables back a couple were drinking beer, their legs intertwined under the table with the man's hand stroking the woman's thigh. They didn't seem to be paying any attention.

'Well,' he continued in a hushed voice, 'this is actually the other thing I'm working on, outside of work hours that is. There are numerous cases of innocent people from Buenaventura going missing – many times after being interrogated by the army – only to be later found in unmarked graves and reported as guerrillas killed in combat.'

Luzma shook her head slowly. She had heard similar stories. She also remembered army officers coming to visit her mum on several occasions and she always seemed scared after they had left. Apparently the army and the paramilitaries didn't like her work against the local gold mining companies that were working illegally on Afro-Colombian land.

'After my mum was disappeared ten years ago I started traveling across our state, Choco, trying to see if I could find out what had happened. I met a lot of other people whose family members had also been taken. Some of the cases were like you said, where innocent people were taken by the army and later claimed to be guerrillas killed in combat. Human rights defenders were particularly at risk,' she said.

'Human rights defenders are definitely targets. But they're also taking completely innocent young boys from poor barrios who they think no-one will miss. They kill them and dress them up in guerrilla fatigues and claim them as a combat kill. There are systems in the army that reward them for the number of enemy combatants they kill.'

'How do people become so sick that they can do something like that?'

'I know, it's hard to understand that they would kill completely innocent people just to get a promotion, a pay rise, extra days of leave or maybe a trip interstate or overseas, but it's the reality, not just in Buenaventura but in lots of other places around the country,' Rafa said.

'Of course they get away with it!' she said indignantly.

'Yeah, I know. Human rights organizations here and in other places around the country have been denouncing these crimes for several years now, but no-one is really paying attention.' He raked his large hand through his thick, curly black hair and leaned back in his chair. 'The US government has given the Colombians over six billion dollars in the past eight years, most of which has gone to the army. Some of that money has gone to the same brigades, like the one operating in Buenaventura, who are committing these crimes.'

'They can't be allowed to get away with this,' she said. 'I wish there was some way to make them pay.'

Rafa motioned for her to be quiet. Behind them the businessmen glanced in their direction. Rafa pulled his chair closer to Luzma.

'I have just been awarded a grant to make a documentary about the human rights abuses in Buenaventura. I want to interview a lot of the family members of the people who have been killed by the army, paramilitaries and guerrillas to give this a human face. I'm trying to see if I can find some lower-ranking officers who are also disgusted with this to allow me to tape their testimony.'

She looked at him with admiration. He was so passionate and brave, just like her mother had been. 'That's amazing. I wish I could help you.'

He studied her for a moment. 'Well, maybe you can,' he said slowly. 'As I said, I have a grant to make this documentary but don't have enough time to do all the preparatory interviews as I work during the day. You know what? Maybe I could pay you a little bit to do some background interviews for me.'

'I'd love to,' Luzma said quickly.

CHAPTER SEVEN

Outside the streets were buzzing with people; couples stood on the corner courting, old women chatted at their front doorsteps, kids played with their toy guns and people roamed the street peddling their wares.

It was hot and humid and sweat trickled down Luzma's neck. Rafa was driving her to meet the people she would be interviewing for his documentary. She opened the window to feel the breeze fan her skin. As he drove, Rafa talked easily, gently asking Luzma questions, finding out a little more about her, getting her to let down her guard.

'Do you have a good relationship with your brother?' Rafa asked.

'Definitely, although he drives me crazy at times. But I suppose since Mum...' She hesitated a moment, 'since Mum disappeared I've felt responsible for him.'

Rafa looked at her as if wondering how to respond. 'What about your dad?'

'He was never really around. He came in and out of our lives. As a kid and a teenager I really looked up to him as he used to tell exciting stories and teach me cool things like self-defence and how to fire a gun. But, after Mum was gone he didn't come back.' She didn't mention that her father had blamed her for her mother being taken.

'Wow. It sounds like you could be quite dangerous with those skills!'

'Yeah, you'd better be nice to me!' she said with a laugh.

'Are you any good?' he asked. 'At self-defence and shooting, I mean.'

'I'm not bad. I used to practise all the time between dad's visits. It was the only time he ever said anything positive to me, so I wanted to try to impress him.' Obviously when a gun had been held to her head it hadn't done any good. Luzma pushed the thought away, turning her attention back to Rafa. 'Tell me about your family?'

'My dad left when I was about seven.' Rafa's face hardened.

'Were you sad when he left?'

'No, I was relieved,' he said, expressionless. 'I thought my mother would be happier without him around to beat her up all the time.'

'I'm sorry.' She gently put her hand on his forearm.

'We all have a story from our past,' he said with a shrug. 'It's how we deal with it in the present that matters.'

They crossed the bridge over to the island and after a while pulled off the main road into some narrow side streets. An old woman stood at the front of a bakery on the corner deep frying *bunuelos* and *empanadas* and a group of people huddled around the counter eating and talking.

'We're entering Los Lleres now. You must never go past this point by yourself,' Rafa said. 'Any work you do without me for the documentary in this area I'll make sure someone picks you up from your house or at the least from this bakery, which is a common meeting spot.'

The street in front seemed a little darker with fewer people.

'I'll be fine, don't worry,' she said offhandedly. She didn't need him to protect her. She was perfectly capable of doing that herself.

'Luzma, you have to be careful here. This is one of the paramilitaries' strongholds. It's where their leader, El Cubano, lives, down on the other end of the street *Piendras Cantan*. But when you're with the nuns who work here or with me you're fine. Today's meeting is in the church. It's close to the entrance of the barrio.'

'Who's El Cubano?'

'He's the most feared person in Buenaventura. People say he controls most of the drugs being transported from this area. Rumor has it that he works for the Norte de Valle Cartel, but no-one knows for sure.' Rafa pulled the car up in front of a large church that was covered with a mural showing a diverse community living together in harmony. Quite different from what Rafa had been describing to her.

'Why is he so feared?'

Rafa looked at her for a while. 'Because he's brutal, and is responsible for much of the killings, torture and disappearances here. They say he has a torture house on the street where he lives, the same street that is guarded by the army.'

The all-too familiar tightening of her chest returned. How could these people get away with so much brutality?

'That's why it's so important to help these people who have been victims of this violence.' Rafa's voice was filled with passion. 'It has to stop.'

'I wish I felt more optimistic that it will,' Luzma said. 'But I've heard about and experienced the paramilitaries, guerrilla and army's abuse my whole life. And you know what? I can barely think of any times where there was any kind of repercussion.'

Rafa and Luzma walked through the church to a large adjoining hall. The room was painfully silent. There were at least thirty people sitting in the circle to the side. They greeted Rafa warmly, but looked at Luzma with suspicion. She didn't blame them. After a while you learn that you can't trust people unless they prove otherwise.

Rafa introduced her and motioned for the woman who was speaking to continue. A shard of light from the high ceiling windows fell across a photo she was holding, as if capturing the image in a spotlight.

'This was my Hector,' the woman said, tears brimming over.

The boy looked younger than Luzma. He was skinny with braided hair falling to his shoulders and a huge goofy smile that filled his face. Her heart went out to the grieving mother.

'This is my boy who they killed,' the woman said. 'On January third this year local army officers arrested Hector and his friends Jose Luis and Juan Camilo,' the woman said, gesturing to the two women hunched over beside her.

One of the women lifted up a photo of her and a young man carrying a baby, joy in their faces. But now her pretty features were lined with deep folds of sorrow. 'This is Juan Camilo a year ago when our baby, Elizabeth was born,' she said, her voice trembling.

The woman beside her had the weathered face of someone who had spent her life working the land. 'This is Jose Luis,' she said, her mouth set tightly as she presented a tattered photo of a young kid with big inquisitive eyes. 'He was only fourteen when they took him.'

Sister Clara, the nun who had helped organize the gathering of victims and their families and the human rights defenders helping them, brought a box of tissues over to the three women. She stood over them, patting their backs, comforting them. Her light grey eyes were moist and her soft features were creased with concern.

'They picked up our boys for no reason, saying they were part of the guerrilla. But they were just innocent kids,' the first woman to speak said, the photo of her son trembling in her hand. 'We asked for them but the army denied ever having arrested them. We looked for months and months until a few weeks ago we got a call from the Attorney-General's office asking us to come in as they'd found some remains in an unmarked grave.' The last words were barely audible as they came out between heaving sobs.

The three women held hands and wept.

Warm tears slid silently down Luzma's face. She felt their pain deep inside her body. For ten years she had travelled around Choco trying to find her mother. She had joined other people whose family members had also disappeared and visited the authorities, the illegally armed groups and even gone to mass graves. She had never found out what had happened. She knew what it felt like to not only lose a love one, but also have no closure. No justice.

'They were our boys in that grave on the outskirts of the city,' the mother of the youngest boy said, fighting back the tears. 'They had to do DNA tests because they were unrecognizable.' Her face distorted in grief as she let out a heart-wrenching wail that echoed around the hall.

'They found out that Hector, Jose Luis and Juan Camilo had all been reported by the army as guerrillas killed in combat,' Sister Clara said.

Rafa leant forward, his fists clenched tightly.

'This is the tenth case this year in Buenaventura. There were twenty-seven cases here last year exactly the same, where the army would take these young boys and kill them and then dress them up as guerrillas and claim they were killed in combat,' Sister Clara said.

'Not to mention the ninety other people who we know have been killed or disappeared because of the paramilitaries or guerrilla this year,' a young woman called Daniela, who was a member of a local Afro-Colombian human rights organization said. She spoke as if she was rallying a crowd, her voice and gestures increasing with each word. 'Fifty of those have been in the past three months, most of them from San Francisco.'

'We've been reporting these types of abuses for years, but nothing has happened and not one single member of the army, paramilitaries or guerrilla has been arrested,' said Mario sitting next to Daniela. He turned his gaze towards Rafa. 'Rafa, you said you think your colleagues in the US might be able to help. What do you have in mind?'

'The US government has given the Colombians six billion dollars in the past eight years, much of which has gone to the army,' Rafa said, looking around the group. 'They have been funding the brigade operating in Buenaventura and its members have benefited from special training trips.'

Everybody in the circle stared at Rafa.

'Do they know what's going on down here and if they do, why the hell do they keep on funding this brigade?' one woman shouted.

'I think some aspects of the government have an idea of what's happening here. But the people in the government who would be appalled by this and could make a difference don't really understand that hundreds, maybe thousands of innocent people are being killed by the Colombian Army.' The passion in Rafa's voice rang out through the church hall. 'We have to make sure those people understand the situation, that they really feel the pain of the mothers, daughters, sisters, brothers, who have lost their loved ones. Just sending them reports isn't enough. I want them to hear from you directly. So I've been talking to some colleagues in human rights organizations in the US and they're eager to help us. I want to do two things; first, make a documentary about these killings in Buenaventura interviewing all of you and others. Second, I'd like to bring some of you out to Washington, DC, to speak directly to members of the Congress and the administration. Would you be interested?'

'I'll do whatever it takes,' the mother of the youngest victim said. She looked at the photo of her son, her chin quivering. 'I stood before his body – or what was left of it – and I promised my Jose Luis that I would not rest until those responsible were behind bars. I don't care what they do to me. I won't stop until I find justice.'

'We can discuss what you'd like included in the documentary today and if people are free during the next few weeks, my friend Luz-Marina is going to help me do some of the interviews as I'm busy with work during the week,' Rafa said, shifting to the side to gesture towards her.

Luzma looked around at all the faces in the room. On some level she felt connected to these people and their pain. She rested her gaze on the woman who'd just spoken. 'We won't rest either until your son's killers are brought to justice.'

Luzma wasn't sure justice actually existed in Colombia. But she dearly wanted to help.

CHAPTER EIGHT

The plump old woman sitting beside Luzma had her pinned tightly to the window. The packed mini-bus bumped along the unpaved roads heading to Los Lleres. A *vallenato* song wailed through the air, the singer's melancholy voice recalling his lost love.

'Hey, Dimples, this is your stop,' a voice bellowed over the *vallenato*. The burly driver turned around to look at her.

She extracted herself from the corner and squeezed past all the people and prepared to step off the bus.

'The church you're after is down that street,' the driver called after her, pointing down a road on the other side of the bus. 'But be careful down that way, two blocks down there and you're in Los Lleres and then...' He shrugged his shoulders.

'Thank you, but I'll be fine.'

The bus doors shut and it pulled away leaving her on the corner in a cloud of dust. Two blocks down and two to the right; that's all she had to walk before she met Sister Clara to begin work on the documentary.

She traversed the first block where a group of teenagers huddled on a doorstep, staring at her as she passed. On the corner of the next block a man stood by the second-floor window looking down. The hairs on her arm stood up. It was quiet and the crunch of the pebbles under her feet was magnified. She picked up her pace.

She was halfway down the second block when an engine throttled behind her. She instinctively jumped to the side, her back hard against the splintered walls of a derelict house. A large black car with dark windows sped around the corner with another one right behind it. Pebbles flew through the air and she raised her hand to cover her face. There was a screech as the second car braked suddenly; backing up to the corner with the same velocity it had arrived with. The first car quickly followed. Luzma pressed her spine harder against the wall. The cars were blocking the entrance to the street she had to walk down.

The back door of the front car opened and legs clad in jeans with white Nike Air runners swung out. Before the feet could touch the ground, two large men from the rear car and one from the front had run to the door. A balloon of smoke floated out of the door. She knew straightaway who it was. El Cubano was exactly how Rafa had described him. He was short and stocky with a protruding gut. His face was pockmarked and a cigar hung between his thick lips.

'Don't worry, boys, I just want to see who our new visitor is,' he said, waving the men off with his small chubby hand. He swaggered towards her, sucking on his cigar and blowing smoke out of one corner of his mouth.

It was only two blocks back to the main road. She eyed the distance. How fast could she move?

'Hello, beautiful, I haven't seen you before,' he said, stepping right before her, while his men stood a few feet away, watching.

She recalled Rafa's words and how this man was responsible for many of the killings and torture in Buenaventura.

'I can't believe I haven't seen you before,' he said. 'Are you living in Los Lleres?'

She shook her head.

'What's your name?' he asked, stepping closer.

She stepped back, repulsed.

'Luz-Marina,' she said coolly.

'Well, beautiful, why don't we go get a drink?'

She wanted to tell him that just looking at him made her want to vomit and she'd prefer to die of thirst than have a drink with him. But that would be suicide. She simply said, 'I can't.'

'Sweetie, I don't think you realize who you're talking to. This is my neighborhood, my town,' he said, drawing out each word in a menacing tone. He blew out another balloon of smoke and bent over to look her in the face.

'Sorry, I must have missed the sign,' she said.

He smiled, apparently not noticing the sarcasm dripping from her voice. 'Well; now you know. Shall we go?'

She kept her hand tightly pinned to her side. She wanted to slap the smile off his repugnant face. But she was clearly alone with him and his men. If she wanted to get out of this safely she needed to control her anger.

'Sorry,' she said, trying to sound sincere, 'I can't today. I have an appointment I must go to and I'm running late.'

Silence hung like the smoke in the air. El Cubano turned and walked back to the car. He said something to his men. They all stared at her, obviously deciding what to do.

She took a deep breath and started walking back up the hill. As she passed she could feel them all watching her. She was sure they were coming for her. As she reached the corner of the main road a bus was passing by. She waved it down.

Once inside the bus, she looked out the window and saw El Cubano staring intently after her. Men like him thought they could have whatever they wanted whenever they wanted. She wished she could wipe that egotistical smile from his face.

CHAPTER NINE

Pablo Ruiz stepped back into his jeep, clenching the cigar between his teeth. The little bitch with the childlike face scuttled away, her braids swishing around her tiny waist. Who did she think she was? He wanted her now. He liked them young and innocent. He drummed his stubby fingers slowly on his leg. Should he take her straightaway? He always got what he wanted one way or another. Some were impressed by his wealth and power; others needed to be taken by force. But, in most cases he preferred when they came by choice. Not through any moral obligation. He loved the taste of power. But, he preferred it when they adored him.

'She's new here,' Carlos said. 'She doesn't know who you are yet. Why don't we give her time to figure that out and then I'm sure she'll be begging to be with you.'

Pablo pulled out a silver box of the finest Cuban cigars from his top pocket and before he even had to think of where he had left his lighter, Carlos had a flame ready. Pablo blew out a long puff of smoke.

'You're right,' he said, winking at his men. 'Let's give her a couple of weeks to make sure she knows who rules this city.'

'So, where to, Boss?' the driver asked.

'The factory,' Pablo replied distractedly. He was staring at himself in the rear-view mirror.

Truth be told, he didn't like mirrors. They forced him to see the pink pockmarks that covered his face. They were a reminder of his childhood when his face was covered with disfiguring pustules. Whenever he thought of that time he was reminded of Ana Maria, the cute little *negra*, much like the girl he had just met, who he had obsessed over for years. But every time he approached her, she looked at him with such raw revulsion that would leave him feeling humiliated. But that little bitch had paid.

The car pulled up in front of the factory. Two of his men stood outside keeping guard.

'Carlos, I want more men guarding the factory,' he said. 'I want to make sure no-one tries to sneak around.'

'I'll get right on it,' the tall, sinewy man said.

Inside the factory Pablo couldn't help but smile at the sight of the submarine. Even he had wondered if they could pull it off. Yet here it was before him in the final stages of construction.

Many other cartels had tried to turn boats into semi-submersible vessels. But no-one else had the audacity and intelligence to get a real Russian submarine.

The submarine had arrived in five modules specially fitted into shipping containers. Now, four months after their arrival, they were welding the final module together. The submarine was sitting on a steel cradle and was surrounded by an elaborate scaffolding system. The three Russian engineers, along with six locals who had been brought in, wore welding masks and heavy leather jackets. Arcs of high intensity white light fizzed as they worked.

'You've nearly done it, Boss,' Carlos said. 'I can remember when you came back from your meeting with the Russian talking about getting a proper submarine. I thought you'd smoked too much!'

Pablo remembered the first meeting he had around eight months ago with Vladimir, the Russian mafia gangster who bought women and drugs from him. It was after the interception of his shipment and he had been desperate, drowning his sorrows in a bottle of *Aguadiente* by the pool of Hotel Gran Estacion. He knew his boss, El Magico, would kill him unless he could come up with an alternate way to ship the cocaine directly to the US and it was proving increasingly difficult.

'Why don't you ship it to the US on a submarine?' Vladimir had asked, swirling the liquid in his glass.

Pablo grunted. 'Colombian drug lords have been using those little semi-submersible submarines to export drugs to Central America since Pablo Escobar's days. My boss isn't interested in selling to the Mexicans. He wants to get directly into the US where the real profit is.'

'What about a full-blown Russian submarine that can dive deep enough to avoid aerial detection and make it directly to the US?'

Pablo laughed. 'My friend, you drink too much vodka. How the hell do you think we'd get a real submarine here?'

'The Colombians have an excess of cocaine and hot women. Russia has an excess of vodka and submarines,' Vladimir said. He took a sip of his drink and continued. 'A lot of old submarines were sent to the scrap yards to be decommissioned. We just happen to own, or, how should I say, have an interest in, several major scrap yards and former state shipping businesses around the country.'

Pablo's interest was piqued. 'You've sold submarines before?'

'Of course. It's a good side business. Many types of people are interested in owning one.'

'Do you think you could actually get me a submarine?' Pablo asked doubtfully.

'In Russia if you have money and connections you can get anything,' Vladimir said, gesturing with his large hands, his gold rings shining. 'My friend, you have money and I have connections.'

This was a way out of this mess. It was a crazy, desperate idea, but it was the best one Pablo had heard. He needed this.

'Can you do this?'

'Don't worry, my friend. You have been very good to me with all the gorgeous women and quality drugs you've provided. I will find what you need.' The Russian raised his glass.

With a clink of glasses and a bottle of Colombia's finest *Aguadiente* the crazy plan had been set in motion.

'I was sweating when we met the Russian the second time after you'd already convinced El Magico to buy the sub,' Carlos said, bringing Pablo back to the present moment.

'You were nervous? How do you think I felt?' Pablo replied. 'It was my balls on the line. If he'd come back empty-handed I would have been a dead man.'

'But what Vladimir found is perfect.' Uncharacteristic enthusiasm lit up Carlos's black eyes.

Pablo had thought the same thing when they had met with Vladimir the second time. He could recall the smug look on the Russian's face.

'You're going to be very impressed with what I've found you,' he had said.

'Tell me,' Pablo responded.

'A Malyutka-class submarine that was sent to one of our scrap yards decades ago. We had a dozen of them, but have sold most of them.'

'A what?'

'It means the little one in Russian. The M-class submarine is a small, single-hulled submarine designed in the beginning of the 1930s to work along the coastline defending naval bases or blockading enemy harbours. They were specifically designed to be transported from one war front to the other. So it's in modules that are easy to assemble.'

'But hold on, how old is this thing?' Pablo asked sceptically.

'It's old. But I've had the diesel engine checked and it's still working. I can get the batteries required to power it,' Vladimir said. 'You'll need Russian submarine experts in areas like heavy electrics, pneumatics and hydraulics and a specialised team to sail it. But, I'm confident that with the right people you can get it working perfectly.'

'How small is it exactly? I need to know how much cocaine it can hold.'

'It's 37 meters and has a 270 cubic meter capacity. I'll leave it to you to figure out how much cocaine you could fit into that,' the Russian said with a smile.

Pablo and Carlos had done the math and realised that could fit at least 7000 tons. It was more than they had ever shipped before and would be equal to well over 200 million US dollars per shipment. Pablo didn't need any more convincing on the deal.

'Pablo.'

Pablo looked up to see Petrov, the head Russian engineer overseeing the build, before him.

'Petrov,' he said, slapping the burly man on the shoulder. 'It looks like you're on track to launch by the end of the month.'

'Welding the modules together has gone smoothly. But if you want this to be in the water in three weeks I'm going to need more help.'

'No problems. Tell me what you need.'

'I need a naval electrician and an additional expert in pneumatics. We have a lot of work to do to get the wiring from the different parts fitting correctly and to get the batteries up and running. Not to mention sea trials. With the limited number of people I have it will take more than a couple of weeks.'

'We don't have longer than a couple of weeks,' Pablo said. 'My boss is not a patient man and we have a lot of cocaine waiting to be shipped. The General also wants us out of the factory as soon as possible.'

'Can you get me the extra men?'

Pablo turned to Carlos. 'Make it happen.'

When the car screeched to a halt in front of the school, Pablo's two kids were waiting for him alone just inside the door. He jumped out of the car without waiting for his bodyguards. Nelly, his four-year-old daughter, came bounding towards him, her face lit up with a toothless grin.

'Papi!' she exclaimed, wrapping her chubby little arms around him.

'My princess.' He scooped her up and planted kisses all over her head. 'I'm so sorry you had to wait for your naughty daddy.'

Fabricio, his six-year-old son remained on the bench, his arms crossed as he looked up.

'Ah, my precious little boy, I'm very sorry,' Pablo said, crouching in front of his son. 'What can Daddy do to make it up to you?'

Fabricio feigned disinterest for a while, before replying, 'You can take us to Disneyland again!'

'Okay, I promise we'll go to Disneyland again in a couple of months,' he said, putting out his hand to shake on the deal.

As he was putting his children in the car, he heard a boy crying nearby. He walked towards the corner with one of his guards quickly following him.

'L-l-leave me alone, I d-d-didn't do anything to y-y-you,' a boy's voice stuttered from around the corner.

'What a little wimp this one is,' a voice responded.

'Can't you speak, stupid?' another boy jeered.

It reminded Pablo of being bullied as a kid, defenceless before the bigger boys who would constantly torment him. These boys needed to learn a lesson. He was driven more out of the lingering scar of his own torment than any real concern for the kid being bullied. He pulled out his gun and turned the corner.

'What's going on here?' He pointed his gun at the four gangly teenagers who were circling their prey.

The boys spun around, eyes wide in shock as they saw the gun and the man that some of them recognized. The victim was a skinny little kid, whose clothes hung limply on his bony frame. He had enormous eyes framed by long eyelashes.

'You come here,' Pablo said.

The little boy responded, shuffling towards him, his entire body shaking.

'What's your name?' Pablo asked.

'J-J-Jair,' the boy muttered.

'Well, Jair, we're going to teach these boys a lesson and make sure they never tease you again. How does that sound?'

The boy looked up at him. 'Good.'

'Marco, teach these boys a lesson to make sure they never touch my little friend Jair again,' Pablo said to his guard.

The guard slammed his fist into one of the boy's faces and then backhanded the one beside him, sending both boys flying to the ground. He picked up another boy and hurled him at the wall. The boy's body smashed into the cement and slumped onto the ground. Finally, he kicked the last boy hard between the legs, leaving him wailing in pain. The little boy at Pablo's side stared at the spectacle.

'If you ever talk badly to Jair again, or so much as touch him, I will come back and slowly kill every last one of you. Am I understood?' Pablo said, pointing the gun at their heads.

'Yes, sir,' the boys said, trembling. A river of urine ran down one boy's leg.

Pablo and his guard left, ushering Jair with them.

'Where do you live?' Pablo asked Jair.

'S-S-San Francisco,' Jair mumbled.

Pablo looked over at Carlos and smiled.

After they'd dropped Jair at the bus stop, Pablo watched the little boy walk away.

'Get him to work for us,' he told his men.

'But he couldn't defend himself if his life depended on it,' one of the guards, Marcos, protested.

'Maybe, but no-one would suspect him of being a spy or of transporting guns or coke. He looks too pathetic,' Pablo said.

CHAPTER TEN

The late afternoon breeze wafted through the open windows of the car. Luzma pulled her braids up onto the top of her head, relishing the coolness on her sweaty neck. Celia Cruz's song 'Te Busco' came on the radio and she smiled at Rafa.

'I love this song,' she said.

Luzma had spent the past fortnight with Rafa working on the documentary and found his passion and commitment to helping people endearing. Despite her efforts to keep her guard up, the gorgeous foreigner was getting under her skin.

Rafa sat in the driver's seat of his parked car facing her, one arm resting on the seat and his hand hanging deliciously close to her bare shoulder. His sleeveless shirt revealed his muscular biceps and shoulders. His skin gleamed in the warm afternoon light. Luzma longed to touch him.

'They say that Celia Cruz's husband died not long after her because he couldn't handle life without her,' he said. 'That's pretty intense.'

She leaned forward a little and his fingertips grazed the nape of her neck, sending a delightful shiver through her body. She held her breath waiting to see what he would do. He slid his finger slowly up her neck and back along her collarbone to her shoulder. The thin strap of her singlet fell down her arm. A wave of heat washed over her. She looked up at him. Her own desire was reflected in his eyes. They sat like that for a long moment. The energy between them was palpable. She leaned closer, craving the touch of his lips. He held her gaze for a moment and then slowly his lips slid softly over hers. His hand caressed the side of her face and down her neck and shoulder and back. Then he pulled her towards him. His chest pressed warmly against her body and she wanted to be closer to him, to feel his heat seeping into her. She touched his muscular arms and back. Their kiss grew more intense.

'Luzma,' a loud voice called out.

They both sat up, startled back to reality. Her grandmother crossed the road towards them, her face tense. They looked at each other, smiling, straightened their clothes and got out of the car.

'Grandma, this is Rafael, who I told you about.'

Her grandmother stared past Rafa into the car. 'Is Jair with you?' Her voice was sharper than normal.

'No, I told you I was going with Rafa to do some more interviews for the documentary this afternoon.' Why was her grandma being so rude to Rafa?

'He hasn't come home. It's nearly eight o'clock and his school finishes at four,' she said, thumbing the beads around her neck. 'He's been coming home late and acting differently these past two weeks, but he's never been this late.'

Luzma had been so busy most afternoons working on the documentary, spending time with Rafa or attending to the sick with Grandma that she hadn't even noticed that Jair had been any different. She thought of all the stories she had heard recently of innocent young men killed and her stomach churned.

'Why don't Luzma and I walk around the neighborhood to see if anyone's seen him and if he's not here we'll drive around until we find him,' Rafa offered.

Grandma looked at him for the first time. She nodded. 'Yes. Thank you. That would be good.'

Rafa pulled out his wallet and handed her a business card. 'This is my cell number so you can call us if he comes home and we'll call you if we find him. Do you have a cell?'

'No, but my sister does and Luzma knows the number,' Grandma said.

Luzma hugged the older woman tightly. 'It will be okay, Grandma. He'll be back soon.' But as the words came out a part of her couldn't shake the image of the photos of those young boys who had been killed.

'I don't know how I didn't notice that Jair has been coming home late,' Luzma said, as they walked towards the football field. 'I'm supposed to protect him.'

'You're a good sister,' Rafa said, squeezing her hand. 'Don't worry. We'll find him.'

The streetlight on the corner flickered and two young boys about Jair's age were throwing pebbles at the light bulb. They looked slightly familiar.

'Hey, do you know my brother Jair?' Luzma asked. 'He's a skinny little kid with an occasional stutter. Jolene is our aunt.'

The boys looked at each other and one of them fiddled with the pebbles in his hand.

'The last time I saw him he was at the old factories in our hiding spot. He goes there a lot,' one of the kids said.

'Yeah, but he's been busy lately with his new friends,' the other boy said, a hint of irritation in his voice.

'What new friends?' Luzma asked.

The boys looked at each other and shrugged. She repeated the question.

'He talks to them after school and sometimes he goes off in that big car of theirs,' one boy said.

'Who are you talking about?' she asked, reaching out to pull the boy towards her so she could make out the outline of his face.

He pushed her hand off his shoulder, but she gripped it.

'I think it's the famous guy they talk about. You know the one who always has lots of men around him, drives big black cars and smokes those enormous smelly cigarettes.'

The energy drained out of Luzma's body, despite the heat she felt cold. She didn't understand. 'That can't be right. My brother would never hang out with him. You must be mistaken.'

'You asked. I'm just telling you what I've seen. Jair talking to that man and the big men that drive around with him and I've seen him get in their car twice,' the boy said. 'That's all I know.'

He had to be talking about El Cubano. Who else could fit that description? But why would Jair get in El Cubano's car? Was he with them now?

'Wait, what's this place in the factory you mentioned?' she asked, following the boys.

'It's nothing,' the boy replied over his shoulder.

'I'll give you ten thousand pesos if you take us there,' Rafa called after them.

Both boys stopped. 'Ten thousand pesos each?'

'Sure.'

Luzma and Rafa followed the two boys through the mangroves on the outskirts of the factories guided only by the moon and the light coming from the main factory that was the farthest away.

'Are you sure Jair might be here?' she asked. 'Why on earth would he be hiding in an old factory at night?'

'This is our hiding spot. Only a few of us know about it. I've seen Jair come here by himself a lot recently. But we don't know if he's here now,' one of the boys said. 'The secret entrance to the factory is up here, underneath the second building. You can only get here during low tide. Otherwise you'd have to swim.'

He led them through knee-deep water underneath the stilts of the second factory building. The mud sucked Luzma's feet deeper down, making it a struggle to keep up with them as they went to the outer corner of the second factory.

'There's one plank marked with a cross above us. You have to move that plank first and then the rest follow,' their guide explained.

Rafa felt above his head and then pushed up and a small line of light fell down across the water. The line expanded as two more planks moved to the side. Rafa hoisted himself up then helped Luzma and the two boys. The room was large and light filtered in from holes in the wall and ceiling. There were rows of timber stacked up about four across and four-storeys high.

'Where do you think he is?' Luzma whispered. She prayed that he was there.

The boys pointed to the far end, where light seeped in from the adjoining factory. 'There's a ladder there that we use to climb up and see into the next factory. They're building this really cool, massive vessel. It looks like a space machine!'

'Jair,' Luzma called out.

'Shhhh. Be quiet. They don't know we're in here,' one of the boys said, heading back the way they had come. 'We'll get in lots of trouble if they find out.'

But Luzma didn't care. She headed towards the adjoining wall with the other factory. If Jair was there she would find him.

There was a ring behind her. She spun around.

'Yes,' Rafa whispered into his phone walking back towards the entrance.

There was a long pause.

'Jair has just got home. He's all right,' Rafa said, putting his arm around her.

The rain fell just as they were reaching the house, soaking them both. Luzma welcomed the cool rain on her face. This was just a misunderstanding. Those boys had confused Jair with someone else.

Aunty Jolene answered the door. She wrapped Luzma and then Rafa in a warm embrace.

'Rafael, I'm pleased to see you're taking care of my niece!' she said with a wink.

Rafa smiled awkwardly. 'Of course, Dona Jolene, anything for you and your family.' He turned to Luzma, 'I didn't realise Jolene was your aunt. We've worked together in the human rights groups for two years now.'

Jair was sitting in the kitchen wedged between Grandma's heavy form and Grandpa's lithe one. His shoulders were hunched and he stared at his hands as they fired questions at him.

'*Flacito!*' Luzma exclaimed rushing towards him and lifting him off his chair with the force of her embrace.

He wrapped his arms tightly around her waist.

'Thank God, you're all right.'

'Yes, thank God he's all right but he almost gave us a heart attack,' Grandma said, her hands on her hips.

Jair gripped tightly onto Luzma's waist. He peeped at Grandma through his long lashes. 'Sorry, Grandma. I j-j-just wanted to help.'

'But, Jair, where did you get this money?' Grandpa asked, tapping his long fingers on the kitchen bench where a small wad of bills lay.

'I h-h-helped some older boys at school. You said we n-n-needed money. I just w-w-wanted to help,' Jair said, glancing at Grandpa, his lower lip shaking.

An alarm bell rang inside Luzma's head. She glanced at Rafa who stood awkwardly in the hallway behind Aunt Jolene. She pulled Jair away from her.

'Who are these boys you've been helping and what have you been doing exactly?'

Jair squirmed away from her. 'They're just boys from school. All I wanted was to help,' he said and ran out of the room in tears.

They all stood in the kitchen staring after him.

Luzma introduced Rafa to Grandpa. Grandma set about making up for her earlier rudeness by insisting he sit down and eat with them. But Luzma's thoughts were elsewhere.

Later that night as she walked with Rafa to the door she said,

'He's lying, isn't he?'

'If we could all go to the show in the park tomorrow I can try to talk to him when he's more relaxed,' Rafa said. 'Maybe he'll be more willing to talk to someone outside the family.'

'What do you think this vessel was that the boys mentioned?'

'I don't know but I'd like to find out. I bet it has something to do with the violence,' Rafa said. 'Mind you, I don't think any of us should go near the factory again. It's far too dangerous.'

CHAPTER ELEVEN

The women's white skirts swished around their legs as their hips swung to the beat of the *currulao* rhythm. The old man playing the marimba smiled broadly, his remaining two teeth protruding. Luzma's hips moved automatically to the rhythm and Jair joined in, smiling as his bare feet thumped the ground.

'*Wuuepa-je*,' the singer screamed, sending the crowd in the waterfront park wild.

'You dance okay for a *gringo*,' Jair said to Rafa.

'Yeah, you've got rhythm.' Luzma circled him closely, grazing his skin as her hips swung from side to side to the beat of the drums.

'Don't forget you said you'd come dancing with me one night.' Rafa's eyes followed her.

'We'll have to do that soon.' She looked up at him. There was a magnetic energy in the small space between them.

The crowd applauded loudly as the group finished their final song.

'Is that the end?' asked Jair, looking sulky.

'For now, but there's another concert we can go to in a couple of weeks,' Rafa reassured him.

The main square by the water was buzzing with people. There were arts and crafts markets, people wandering around selling food, phone cards and drinks. They passed the lighthouse in the center of the park where a couple was making out on the white stairs. Rafa looked at them and then winked at Luzma.

They stopped in front of a man selling ice cream out of a mobile cart. They each got a coconut ice cream and weaved their way through the crowd, passing the mini-bars that were crowded with couples trying to speak over the blasting music. They reached the waterfront and followed Rafa down a narrow concrete pathway leading out to a breakwater that held the sea back from the city. They sat at the furthest point, their feet dangling in the water. Luzma's toes tickled as the water swirled around them. She sat shoulder to shoulder with Rafa and it sent a warm tingle down the side of her body.

'So what do you think of Buenaventura?' Rafa asked Jair, who was sitting to his right.

'This part is pretty cool. But not everything is like this. I miss our home,' Jair said, gazing out at the water as he licked his ice cream.

'And what's school like? Do you have many friends?'

'No, the boys used to always tease me.' Jair stopped and smiled a moment. 'But not anymore.'

'I used to get bullied as well,' Rafa said. 'I never really fit in. I was always different.'

Jair looked at him quizzically. 'You got beat up?'

'Lots!'

'What did you do to stop it?'

'Some things I regret now. I got mixed up in a gang and did a lot of dumb stuff,' Rafa said.

'What sort of stuff?' Jair asked.

'Dumb stuff like petty crime, drugs, being a bit of a thug.'

Luzma looked at Rafa in disbelief. She couldn't imagine him in that kind of world. It made her respect him even more because he had changed the direction of his life and she was touched that he was willing to share this to help Jair.

'Wow, but did it stop the other kids beating you up?' Jair asked eagerly.

'Sort of, but it cost me dearly.'

'How?' Jair asked.

Rafa glanced at Luzma and then swallowed hard. He hesitated. 'I lost people I loved, including my girlfriend and a friend.'

'How did you lose them?' Jair persisted.

Luzma knew she should tell Jair to stop being so nosey but she also wanted to know.

Rafa looked straight at Jair. 'They were killed. That's what happens in those types of gangs.'

Luzma stared at Rafa. He hadn't talked about this before.

'I'm sorry. That's awful,' Jair said.

'Enough about me. What about you? You said the kids don't bully you anymore. How'd you manage that?' Rafa asked, nudging Jair with his elbow.

'Yeah, they're scared of me now,' Jair said, smiling and sitting up a little straighter. 'Two weeks ago a group of the big kids were picking on me and being really mean. Then suddenly out of nowhere this man arrived and stopped them. They all looked so scared when they saw him. Then this big man with him beat up the mean kids. You should have seen it. He really made them understand what it's like!'

'Oh, cool,' Rafa said. 'So who was this guy?'

'His name is Pablo. I think he is pretty important as he always has a whole car full of men following him around and everybody seems to do what he says. Since I've been hanging out with him everybody leaves me alone.'

'El Cubano,' Luzma whispered.

Rafa looked at her and nodded. 'You've been hanging out with this guy?' he asked casually.

'Yeah,' Jair hesitated, looking at Luzma.

She tried to fake nonchalance.

'It's actually him who's been paying me to do some work. Only he said it would be better if I didn't tell other people that I was working for him. I'm sorry, Sis, I didn't mean to lie.'

Luzma shifted her glance and stared out at the horizon. She nodded because she didn't think she could speak without losing it.

How could he work for the same sort of people who had taken their mother? How could he put himself in that kind of danger?

'So what sort of work are you doing for this guy?' Rafa asked.

'It's pretty simple. I just have to hang out with another boy in the street leading up to the factory and take note of anyone going up there. It's very easy work and he pays really well. I've been able to buy food for the family,' Jair said, proudly puffing out his chest.

'How dare you bring money into our house from the paramilitaries,' Luzma exploded. 'I'd prefer to starve than have you do this!'

Jair stared at her. 'What are you talking about?'

'The man you're working for is El Cubano, the head of the paramilitaries in Buenaventura. The most feared person here,' she shouted at him. 'You could be killed any moment for doing this work.'

'No, y-y-you're wrong. He's a nice man,' he said. 'Why are you angry at me when all I'm trying to do is help our family?'

Lightning cracked across the sky and the dark clouds rolled closer towards them.

'He's just like the people who took our mother and now you're helping him,' she said, shaking with anger.

'Jair, this happens a lot here,' Rafa said. 'Pablo Ruiz, or El Cubano, as he is known, recruits young boys to do simple jobs like watching over the neighborhood and taking messages and packages to people. Like you said, it seems harmless, easy money. But it doesn't stop there. Slowly these young men get more and more involved and before they know it they're carrying a gun and then they've killed someone. I'm sure Pablo can be very charming and he helped you with the bullies, but trust us; he has a very dark side. He is feared throughout Buenaventura because of the number of people he has killed and tortured. He's not a person you want to have anything to do with.'

Jair stared at them, tears brimming in his eyes. 'Are you sure?'

'Yes, we're sure,' Rafa replied.

'I'm sorry, Luzma. I didn't know. Please don't be angry with me.'

Luzma took a deep breath. 'I'm not angry with you. I'm worried about you. Please, *Flacito,* promise me that you won't have anything to do with him anymore.'

Suddenly the skies burst with torrential rain. Rafa stood and held out his hand to pull Luzma up. But she didn't move.

'Promise,' she repeated.

Jair nodded. His wet clothes clung to him, making his small body appear even more fragile. How had she let this happen? They used to talk about everything, but somehow he'd been working for the paramilitary boss and she had never even realized. If Mum were watching them from heaven she would surely be heartbroken.

CHAPTER TWELVE

Suddenly the front door slammed open.

'What are you doing home?' Luzma asked, startled as Jair walked through the door. It was only two pm.

'Where's Aunty Jolene?' he asked, eyes darting around the house.

'She's at another one of her meetings. We're preparing a letter about the abuses here to send to the national government and the US,' she said, distracted by Jair's fidgeting. 'What's wrong?'

'We need to find Aunty now!' His voice was breathless.

'Jair, sit down and tell me what's wrong,' she said, sitting on the couch and pulling him down beside her.

He began to rock back and forth. 'I tried to avoid him like you said. I promise I did. Please don't be angry at me.' He glanced up at her and shifted his gaze to the floor.

A knot formed in her stomach. He was talking about El Cubano.

'I'm not angry at you, *Flaco*, but please tell me what's wrong.'

'Ever since you and Rafa told me about who Pablo Ruiz is I've tried to avoid him. I've been leaving school early every day so I wouldn't see him. But today one of his men came to get me at lunch. They said Pablo wanted to see me and it wasn't a good idea to let him down. I was really scared.' His rocking grew faster.

Luzma leant forward and wrapped his little body in a hug. These men like El Cubano thought they ruled the world and everybody in it.

'Thank God you're all right,' she said.

Jair pulled back and looked at her, his eyes wide. 'But we have to do something before they kill Aunt Jolene.'

'What are you talking about?' she asked, gripping his shoulder.

'They s-said that they had to get r-r-rid of those people who were causing problems for them in San Francisco. They said they had to k-k-kill them. They named Aunty Jolene,' Jair said.

The tightness in her stomach rose up to her chest. 'Explain exactly what happened.'

'They took me to a house to see Pablo. He told me he needed me to try to sneak into community meetings and find out what people were talking about and report back to him. I told him I couldn't, but he got really angry and told me I owed him. Then Carlos, that tall skinny guy who is always with him, came in. He said General Ordonez was at the house and demanding to speak to him immediately. They shoved me out the door as a big man in an army uniform walked in. I stood out the front of the door trying to think of a reason that Pablo would accept so I didn't have to work for him anymore. Then I heard Pablo and the General shouting at each other. They were saying that these human rights defenders in San Francisco were poking around the factory and causing problems. The General said if his bosses in Bogota found out about what they were doing in the factory he would lose his job, his chance of becoming Commander in Chief and he might even go to prison. Pablo shouted at him something like, "screw your job, we'll lose millions of dollars and I'll be killed".'

Jair was speaking so fast Luzma could barely keep up.

'Then they said they had to get rid of all of the troublemakers. The General said, "The first person we should kill is Jolene Cuesta. She's responsible for half these problems. Get rid of her straightaway.' Jair trembled as he spoke. 'We have to stop them, Luzma, or they're going to kill Aunty Jolene!'

Luzma's head was spinning. 'Do they know you heard them?'

'No, after I heard that I ran away and came home as fast as I could. What are we going to do?' he asked, tugging her hand.

'Do they know she's your aunt?'

'I don't think so,' Jair said. 'I never told them.'

'We have to find her. Let's go!' Luzma said, heading for the door.

They walked to the corner where a man had a cart with junk food and mobile phones attached by a cord. She grabbed Jair's hand and kept him close to her. Two men stood at the entrance to the general store across the road. Were they paramilitaries?

She gave the man on the corner two coins to use the phone and dialled Jolene's number. *Please pick up.* The phone rang until it went to voicemail. Rafa was still in Cali for a two-day human rights conference and wouldn't be back until that night. She tried him nevertheless, but it went straight to his message bank. She glanced at the men on the corner. They were glaring at them. She pulled a scrunched up piece of paper out of her bag and dialled Diana's number. She answered.

'Diana, it's Luzma. Do you know where Aunty Jolene is? It's very important.'

'No,' Diana said. 'Actually I tried to find her this morning but she hasn't been answering her phone all day and she's not in the church or the other places they normally meet. What's wrong?'

Luzma could sense the men on the corner behind them watching. Jair pulled at her hand. 'Where is she? What are we going to do?'

Her mind raced. Grandma was at a patient's house but she didn't know where it was and she had no phone. Grandpa was still selling the fish he had caught during the day and she didn't know exactly where he was either.

'Luzma, are you there? Are you okay?' Diana asked.

'Diana, can you meet me in twenty minutes at the main government building in the city?'

'Yes, I'm in the center now. I'll see you there.'

Diana's perfect features were furrowed as Luzma finished telling her what Jair had heard. The tall government building stretched above them and they huddled on the steps speaking in whispers. It was hard to hear over the top of the blasting horns, the constant chatter and the music pounding from the corner café.

Diana tried to call Jolene again but there was still no response.

'What should we do?' Luzma asked. 'We can't tell the army or the police and I can't get hold of anyone. We have to do something before they kill her. It sounds like they were planning to do it straightaway.'

Diana bit her nails. 'Do you think the local government will help?' she asked, pointing up the stairs to the building.

'Well, I've heard Rafa say that some people have protection programs when they're threatened. I don't know who the right person to ask is, but someone in there has to know.'

She wished Rafa were there, he dealt with people who were threatened all the time. But she couldn't wait until that night; she needed to do something now.

Inside the building the two receptionists stared at them blankly when they asked for the protection program.

'Who do we talk to if someone is in danger?' Luzma asked impatiently.

'The police or the army,' the first receptionist said, as though she was speaking to a five-year old.

'I don't want to ask them. Who in the government can help?'

'Well, you could try speaking to the government representative, Viviane Moran,' the other receptionist said.

They took a rickety little elevator to the twelfth floor. It moved at a painfully slow pace.

'Luzma, I don't know what the paramilitaries are doing in the factory in San Francisco, but I'm worried,' Diana said.

Luzma looked at her. 'You mean about Jolene?'

'Yes, but also about my boyfriend, Mauricio,' she said. 'He's an electrician in the army. A couple of weeks ago he was recruited by the General to work in the factory. He won't tell me what's going on. He said it would put me at risk. But he's really nervous all the time. He wants to get out but doesn't know how to.'

The doors opened and they walked into a maze of small cubicles.

'I'm sorry,' Luzma said. 'Let's figure this thing out with Jolene and then we'll see what we can do to help your boyfriend.'

They asked for Viviane Moran and were shown to a sterile waiting room with whitewashed walls and cold metal chairs.

'Do you want me to come in with you or should I keep trying to call people?' Diana asked.

'Best if you keep trying to get a hold of her,' Luzma replied.

A woman came out and motioned for them to follow her. Jair and Luzma were led into a large room with a spectacular view out to the ocean. A tall buxom woman with a tight leopard-print silk blouse and long black hair sat behind the desk.

'What seems to be the problem?' The representative motioned for them to sit down.

'My aunt needs protection or she's going to be killed,' Luzma said.

The woman arched her perfectly plucked eyebrows. 'How do you know your aunt is going to be killed?'

'Jair, my brother, heard them planning to kill her. Can you help us?'

The woman looked intently at Jair. 'Who and what exactly did you hear?'

Jair repeated what he'd heard. She jotted down notes and then put down her pen and began to drum her long red fingernails on the table.

'Can you help Aunty Jolene?' Jair asked.

'Well, I will surely try,' the woman said. 'Tell me, Jair, did anyone else hear this conversation?'

'No, just me. Don't you believe me?' he asked.

'Of course I believe you. I just want to understand all the facts. Have you told anyone else?' she asked, adding 'So I can coordinate with them.'

'No,' Luzma responded, starting to feel irritated by this woman. 'Look this is an emergency. Are you going to help us or not?'

'Of course I'll help you. I need you to write down your aunt's address and yours as well and your phone numbers. Then I suggest you go wait at home. We will have someone come to talk to you and your aunty about different ways we can offer protection.'

Luzma didn't trust this woman. She didn't seem like she genuinely wanted to help them. Maybe she should find another way to help her aunt instead.

'I can't protect her unless you tell me where you all live,' the woman insisted. 'And it sounds like she needs protection urgently.'

She was right. Luzma couldn't afford to wait. What other choice did she have? She wrote down their address and handed it to her. 'Please come today. This is an emergency.'

'Most certainly,' the woman replied with a nod and then showed them to the door.

CHAPTER THIRTEEN

Aunty Jolene fixed the bright yellow and blue African-print scarf around her head, ignoring her sister's pleas for her to leave Buenaventura. Luzma was relieved she was safe, but she would not be for long if she stayed.

'Grandma's right,' Luzma said. 'You need to leave before they get to you. You heard what Jair told you. They want you dead.'

'My dear, we can't constantly spend our lives running away,' Jolene said. 'Our people have been ripped from their land and community too many times. We need to be connected to those two things and this has become my community. The people here need me. I won't leave them.'

Grandma shook her head. 'What use are you to the community if you're dead?'

'Come now, *Yole*. It's not that bad. Luzma and Jair have organized protection for me.'

'What does that actually mean in reality?' Teo, her husband asked, his arms folded across his chest. 'I heard of one man who was given a bulletproof vest and then the Guerrilla killed him to get the jacket.'

Jolene laughed. 'Hopefully they'll come up with something a bit more useful for me.'

'What if they don't do anything at all?' Luzma asked. She didn't trust the woman they'd spoken to. She hadn't seemed that interested in Jolene's safety. 'They said for us to stay at home and they would send someone, but it's nearly 9pm and no-one has come.'

'I think we all just need to relax,' Jolene said, patting Luzma's arm. 'Things don't happen that quickly here. I will keep a low profile in the meantime.'

There was a knock on the door. Was that someone from the government's protection program, or was it the paramilitaries coming for Jolene?

'I'll get it,' Teo said, heading for the door.

He returned with Rafa in tow. He looked even more handsome than usual, a white linen shirt unbuttoned at the top. His curly black hair fell across his face. Luzma had been so preoccupied she hadn't gotten ready for their date. Now she didn't feel right going out.

Rafa smiled at Luzma and kissed her on the cheek. He was wearing the cologne she loved. He greeted each of the family members, giving Jair a high five.

'Hi, sorry I missed your calls,' Rafa said to Luzma. 'Is everything all right?'

'I'm sorry, Rafa. I don't know if I can go out tonight.' He looked disappointed so she quickly added. 'I really want to go, but we've had a big problem today and I need to stay home with my family.'

'Don't be silly, Luzma,' Jolene said. 'You're young. You should go out and dance and enjoy life. Leave the worrying to when you're our age.'

'But I should stay in case they come.'

'Yeah, don't worry,' Rafa said. 'If it's inconvenient we can do it some other time.'

'Jolene's right,' Grandma said. 'There's no need for you to stay around here. Nothing is happening tonight. We're just going to sleep.'

'Are you sure?'

'Yes, get out of here and have a dance for us,' Jolene said, motioning her towards the door.

Luzma smiled at the thought of dancing with Rafa. 'Give me fifteen minutes so I can get ready.'

The music was so loud it pulsed through Luzma's chest. Bodies pressed together on the dance floor, limbs intertwined, hips swung sensuously and sweaty skin gleamed in the low orange light.

Rafa held her hand, keeping her close to him as they squeezed past the overflowing dance floor and the tables against the wall where couples huddled together.

They reached the bar and Rafa ordered two beers. The cold drink was welcome in the sticky heat.

Rafa looked at her for a long moment and then bent over, brushing her hair away from her face and bringing his mouth to her ear. 'You look very beautiful tonight.'

His breath was hot against her skin. She wished he would kiss her neck, but he pulled back. The music, the heat, the beer, the dim light and the electric currents between them cast away her usual reserve with men.

'Salio el Sol', one of her favorite *regatton* songs came on. She smiled, motioning towards the dance floor. The good thing about regatton was that it was meant to be danced as close together as possible. Rafa pulled her towards him until their bodies were squeezed together. Her hips and torso circled sensuously, bringing him with her. His hand was firm against her lower back, his finger at the base of her spine. Their bodies moved together as one.

The song changed to 'La Magia de tus Besos' by Grupo Niche. He kept her close in the true romantic salsa style. She wrapped her arms around him, feeling his muscular back. It was said that in salsa no-one should be able to tell where one body ended and the other began.

'You're very good,' she said, looking up at him.

He smiled. 'You mean for a *gringo*.'

'A Dormir Juntitos' begun to play. He pulled her closer, his fingers at the top of her buttocks. She curled into his body, her head on his chest as they moved to the *merengue* beat. She wanted to be closer. She slid one hand down his back, pulling him into her. He was hard. It excited her more. Her chest rose heavily, her breasts pushing against the low cut top. He pulled her in tight.

The *regatton* 'Esta Noche de Travesura' came on. Their bodies began to grind together. She looked up at him. His eyes were hungry. He brushed his hand down the side of her face and then leant down and kissed her, softly to start with and then more intensely. She ran a hand through his hair and the other down the muscles of his back. A desperate longing surged between them. They grasped at each other, unable to get close enough. Her breath was sharp and shallow. She kissed the smooth skin of his neck. He smelt deliciously intoxicating.

'Do you want to come to my apartment?' he whispered.

CHAPTER FOURTEEN

Rafa's muscular arm was wrapped around Luzma and her head lay on his chest. Her naked body was curled into his, their legs entwined. The bedside lamp cast a warm glow over the small room. The soft breeze rippled the curtains, revealing the moon. The heat of his body soaked into her skin and filled her with a calm bliss. Her skin tingled with pleasure as he slowly stroked her side. If paradise existed this was it.

The opening beats of Shakira's *Tortura* broke the blissful silence. They both looked up, disoriented. It was the ringtone of Rafa's cell phone.

'Surely they can wait,' Rafa said.

She wanted him again. It was an insatiable hunger she had never experienced.

'I definitely think they can wait,' she said and began to kiss his neck then his chest. His stomach quivered as her mouth worked downwards.

The ring of his phone disturbed the air again. He groaned.

'Seriously? Who is that? It's the middle of the night!' He reached for his jeans that were discarded beside the bed and pulled out the phone.

Luzma laughed at his dishevelled look and dazed voice as he answered the phone.

'Yes, she's here. Is everything all right?'

A cold chill ran up her back as his eyes widened in shock at whatever the person had told him.

'Who is it?' she asked, sitting up to face him. 'What's wrong?'

'It's your grandmother,' he said, hesitating to pass her the phone.

She snatched it from him. 'Grandma, what's wrong?'

The line was silent and then Grandma began to sob. Rafa touched her shoulder, but his skin felt cold now.

'Is it Jair?' she asked, but she already knew the answer.

'They just came for him. They took him away. I tried, I really tried to stop them, but they pulled out a gun and told me that they needed to talk to Jair,' Grandma said, her usually strong voice now wheezing and trembling. 'I tried everything, but they dragged him away from us and when your grandpa tried to stop them they hit him to the ground. They threatened to kill him and Jair if we moved.'

'Who, Grandma? Who took Jair?' Luzma's fist was clenched tightly around the phone.

'The paramilitaries, we think, or maybe army officers out of uniform. They refused to identify themselves,' Grandma said crying. 'They wanted you as well. They said they needed to bring you both in for questioning. They didn't believe me that you weren't here so they ransacked Jolene's house.'

The tears streamed down Luzma's face. She had been making love while they took her brother. Maybe if she had been there they would have taken her instead.

'What did they say?' She began to throw on her clothes.

'They just said they needed to talk to him.' Grandma tried to catch her breath through her sobs. 'But as they were leaving I heard them say to Jair that they knew that both he and you had reported them to the government.'

Luzma's muscles stiffened. *How did the paramilitaries know that we had told the authorities what Jair had heard? Had Diana told them? Or was it the government officer? They were the only possibilities.*

Luzma thought of her mother. She remembered the police officer telling her grandpa that the first 24 hours were crucial once someone disappeared or was taken. After that the chances of finding them alive were slim. A wave of adrenaline pumped through Luzma's body.

'I'm going to report this straightaway. Rafa and I will make sure nothing happens to him.'

'No, Luzma, you have to hide or they'll take you as well,' her grandma said.

'I'm going to get him back, I promise. I'm with Rafa so I'll be safe. I'll call you later to let you know what I've found out. I love you and Grandpa and Aunty Jolene,' she said and then hung up.

'I have to go to the army headquarters and report this,' she said, putting on her shoes.

'Do they know who took him and why?'

'The paramilitaries or maybe the General's men.' She could barely speak as she was shaking uncontrollably. 'They know what Jair heard and that we reported them.'

'The local government official you spoke to told them?' Rafa asked. He shook his head slowly. 'Bastards! The paramilitaries and guerrilla corrupt everyone! Who the hell are people meant to trust?'

'Either her or Diana, but I doubt Diana told them.' Tears ran into her mouth as she spoke. 'It was my suggestion to go to the government. If anything happens to him it's my fault.'

Rafa held her and stroked her hair. 'It's not your fault. You were just protecting your aunt.'

She pulled away from him. 'We have to do something now. Can you call all your contacts in the US and ask for their help?'

'It's nearly two in the morning. I will call the US Embassy and my colleagues in the human rights organizations in the US first thing in the morning. I promise you they will call the local and national government about this until they get an answer.'

Luzma thought about when her mother was taken. Her father had always blamed her. He said if she had not told her mother what the paramilitary officer had done to her, her mother would never have gone to the paramilitary leader to confront him and then she would never have been taken. Her grandparents had reassured her that she was taken for her political advocacy, but Luzma had never really believed them. And now Jair was taken because of her. She replayed the words of the policeman they had spoken to about her mother's disappearance over and over in her head. *The first twenty-four hours are crucial when someone is taken.*

'I can't wait until the morning. Every minute counts. I'm going to the army headquarters.'

'You can't do that. They're probably involved and they might want you as well.'

She didn't tell him that they were specifically looking for both Jair and her.

'I can't sit around and wait for seven hours for you to call the US. I have to do something now. I have to try to make the army do something about this. They have to know if they don't we'll create problems for them internationally.' She didn't really know if what she was saying made sense, but she had to do something. She extricated herself from Rafa's arms and walked to the door.

'Luzma, that's dangerous,' he protested, grabbing her hand and spinning her around. 'The army is probably involved. You know that. If you show up there they'll just take you. It's too risky.'

'Rafa, I've got to do something. I'm not waiting until the morning. Would you prefer I go to Los Lleres and ask El Cubano where Jair is?'

'Luzma.' His head was cocked to the side, his eyes imploring.

She pulled away and turned to the door. She had to keep going. Her brother needed her.

She was closing the door when Rafa caught her hand.

'There's no way you're going by yourself,' he said. 'If I can't convince you not to go, then I'll come with you. They're not going to take you or hurt you in front of a US citizen. That would create a diplomatic nightmare.'

Army officers with automatic rifles in their hands, slipped in and out of the shadows cast by the enormous lights around the army base. Nobody spoke and in the stillness of the night each sound was magnified. Luzma and Rafa hid alongside the building in the shadows. But if they stepped out they would be caught in the strobe lights and one of the dozens of men guarding the perimeter would see them. There would be no going back.

Where was Jair right now? Luzma imagined his stuttering, squeaky voice begging his captors to let him go. Were they hurting him? The thought was unbearable. She had to do something, regardless of the risk. She took several steps forward into the light. In a matter of seconds two guns were pointed at her chest. Rafa followed her.

'Who are you?' one of the men at the entrance asked.

'Luz-Marina Cuesta,' she replied, squinting against the light.

'We are here to report the kidnapping of my brother, Jair Cuesta.'

The light shifted to Rafa.

'I'm Rafael Wilson. I am an American citizen and I work for Peace Brigades International.'

'It's 2.30 in the morning. Come back at eight am,' the man said.

Luzma couldn't wait until tomorrow morning. Who knew what Jair's captors would do to him between now and then. 'If something is not done immediately my brother could be killed,' she said.

'Come back tomorrow morning and we will see what we can do,' the officer said, enunciating each word slowly as if she didn't understand.

'Sir, this headquarters belongs to the 13th and 14th brigades of the Colombian Army, doesn't it?' Rafa asked.

'What's that got to do with anything?' the officer asked impatiently.

'Well, sir, you might be aware that the United States Government has funded this army brigade for the past five years,' Rafa said, pausing a moment before continuing. 'The US Government would be interested to know the number of cases of forced disappearances where the army has been allegedly directly or indirectly involved. I think that it would be in your interest to be doing all you can to solve these cases. Don't you?'

There was silence. No-one spoke. No-one moved.

Finally, the officer said, 'Fine, Mr Wilson. I will check with my supervisor to see if he has any information. But I doubt it.'

The man disappeared behind an iron gate. After ten minutes he emerged. 'It appears you are very lucky. General Ordonez happens to be in the headquarters and said he was very interested to meet you.'

Wasn't it the General who Jair had heard saying Jolene must be killed?

The officer motioned for them to pass through security, then the heavy iron gate swung open and they were led to an office inside. The scraping sound of the metal lock sliding closed sent a chill through Luzma's body.

'Identification,' the man in the office ordered.

Rafa slid his passport across the bench and Luzma handed over her ID card.

The man studied them. 'Go ahead.'

They followed one of the officers down a pathway to the large concrete building. On every corner there was a tower with several snipers in place. The night air was mild but Luzma shivered through her thin sweater. They were led into an austere reception area with an officer sitting behind a grey metal desk.

'The General has said he will see these two,' the officer accompanying them said.

The desk officer picked up the phone, punched a number and simply said, 'They're here.'

The room looked like a prison cell, with no windows and nothing but cold cement walls, metal chairs and a matching desk. There were only two doors, the one they'd just entered that was now shut and blocked by the officer accompanying them and a door behind the desk where another stony faced officer stood, his hand firmly wrapped around his gun.

The side door clicked open and the officers stood to attention as a tall, well-built man with short sandy hair and matching moustache strode through the door. He stopped in front of them, his body erect and rigid.

'You must be Luz-Marina Cuesta,' he said, his icy grey eyes narrowing. 'I am General Ordonez.'

Luzma thought of all the stories she had heard about innocent young boys being killed by corrupt sections of the army. Was this man involved in those and in Jair's kidnapping?

He turned to Rafa with a thin smile and said in English, 'And you must be the American.' He shook Rafa's hand and added something Luzma didn't understand. 'I completed my military training in America. You have many fine teachers.'

'We are here to report the kidnapping of my brother, Jair Cuesta,' Luzma said. 'He is only twelve years old and was taken tonight by armed men whom we believe to be the paramilitaries.'

'I'm very sorry to hear that. You should file a formal report with our desk officer.' The General moved closer to Luzma. 'Why exactly do you think he was taken? Is he involved with the paramilitaries or the guerrilla?'

Luzma's face flushed. She fought the urge to slap him. 'My brother has nothing to do with those animals. He's an innocent young boy.'

'I'm sure he is,' the General said coldly. 'Did one of you witness the boy being taken?'

'My grandmother and aunt did. They took him from my aunt's place where we are living.'

'And where were you at the time?' he asked.

'That is not relevant,' Luzma said impatiently. 'What is important is that Jair was kidnapped and we want to see if you know anything about it.'

The General's back seemed to stiffen. 'Why do you think we would have any information about the paramilitaries kidnapping the boy? This is the first we have heard about it.'

'How can you be so sure? Don't you need to check with your men?' Luzma asked.

The General's eyes narrowed, his gaze fixed on Luzma. 'Miss Cuesta, I am a General with twenty-five years of experience working in the armed forces. I don't need your help to do my job.'

'It's important that I let you know that the US Government will be informed about this case and will be paying close attention to make sure Jair doesn't turn up in a ditch dressed as a guerrilla apparently killed in combat,' Rafa said.

'Are you accusing my men?' the General asked, taking a step closer to Luzma and Rafa.

'No, just letting you know that we will be paying close attention to this case,' Rafa answered, staring straight at the General.

'Good. Now you two take care. Buenaventura is an extremely dangerous place.'

CHAPTER FIFTEEN

Luzma and Rafa sat in the car in a dark alleyway on the outskirts of the military controlled zone. The area was eerily quiet compared to the usual buzz of Buenaventura. Luzma thought of one of the last conversations she had had with her mother. It was as if her mother had known what was coming.

'If anything ever happens to me, you'll look after your brother, won't you?' she had said, touching Luzma's cheek. 'He's lucky to have such a strong, brave sister to take care of him.'

'Luzma, we need to get out of here,' Rafa said, bringing her back to the present.

'No, we have to figure out what we can do right now to get Jair back.'

'I understand how worried you are, I really do,' Rafa tried to pull her towards him, but she resisted. 'But you can't do anything right now that won't put you in serious danger and I won't let that happen.'

'I'm not going to let another one of my family be killed. I am responsible for what happened to my mother. I'm not going to let anything happen to Jair, of all people.'

'Luzma I've also lost someone I loved. My girlfriend overdosed on drugs when she was only nineteen. I got her into that fucked-up world of drugs and gangs. It was my fault and I have to live with that. I've tried to make up for all the shit I did as a teenager, but I haven't wanted to care so much about someone again. Until you.'

Luzma felt herself softening. 'I know how much you want to protect people and especially me and I love that in you, but ...

The sudden sound of the iron gate at the headquarters cranking open stopped their conversation. Rafa's car was tucked away in a dark alleyway around the corner from the barracks. The bright lights that shone on the entrance to the headquarters highlighted two army officers standing to attention and saluting. As the car pulled out and turned onto the street adjacent to the alleyway, the General leaned out of the passenger window to say something to the guard.

'Rafa, it's the General. We have to follow him.'

Rafa turned to look at her. 'Luzma, are you crazy? Do you want to get us killed?'

Luzma knew the risk she was taking and also putting Rafa at risk. She cringed. Her gut instinct was telling her that she needed to follow the General.

'I'm sorry. I would go by myself if I could but I can't drive. The General is involved, I just know it. We need to follow him to find Jair.'

The General's car turned off the main road onto the street that led into San Francisco. Rafa kept his distance, hiding behind a large truck.

'He's going to San Francisco,' Luzma said. 'Do you think he's going back to Aunty Jolene's house?'

'If the paramilitaries are after you, the last place we're going right now is into San Francisco. They're crawling all over the place.'

'Rafa, we don't have a choice.' Luzma was determined. She wasn't going to give up on Jair.

Rafa drove past the entrance to the main road.

'Where are you going? We have to keep on following him. He might be going back to Jolene's house or to wherever they have Jair.'

'I said no, Luzma. I'm not putting you in that kind of danger.'

Luzma opened the door.

Rafa grabbed her hand. 'What are you going to do, jump out while the car is moving? You're intelligent, Luzma, use your head, if you get yourself caught you're of no use to Jair.'

Luzma stared at him intently. 'If you want to protect me then come in with me because I'm going in there with or without you.'

Rafa grunted. 'Fine.'

He turned at the next entrance and started winding through the back streets into the neighborhood. The streets were completely dark, eerily illuminated by the light of the moon. Luzma strained to get a glimpse of the General's car, but couldn't see it. The night was still and the sound of the car's engine and the tyres against the gravel street was amplified.

Rafa slowed the car as they reached the corner of Aunty Jolene's street. Her house was several blocks away to the right. 'I don't see his car or any lights,' he said.

Luzma yearned to run to the house, to be with her family.

'Luzma, we're going back,' Rafa said.

'Please just drive to the end of this street where we can see the river and the factory and see if we can find the General's car and then we'll leave.'

Rafa slowly edged forward, stopping at each corner to look around and check that no-one was there. Finally, they came to the end of the street on the corner of the river and the mangroves. The factory was several football fields away. The General's car was parked in front of the factory. The lights were still on and they lit up several men who were patrolling in front.

Rafa pulled his car up beside an old fishing boat that had been dragged up onto shore. The boat and the shadows offered a hiding spot. He killed the engine. They sat watching, waiting, but, for what Luzma was not sure. All she knew was that her intuition told her that she would find out what had happened to Jair there. The lights of the General's car were cut, leaving only small shards of light escaping from the main factory. The doors opened and three people got out and walked towards the factory entrance.

The solid walls of Rafa's car seemed secure compared to the dark unknown outside. For Jair's sake she had to follow the General. He had the answers, she was sure.

'I'm going into the adjoining factory through that passage way that Jair's friend showed us,' she said.

Rafa grabbed her arm, his grip firm. 'Luzma, don't be an idiot. That's too dangerous. The place is swarming with paramilitaries and they'll kill you if they find you snooping around there.'

'All the guards are surrounding the main factory, but here, to the outside edge of the second factory along the mangroves, is clear. Once inside I can hear what is going on. I want to know where they are keeping Jair.'

She prised Rafa's hand from her arm and slipped out the door. If she walked through the mangroves to the side of the factory she should be able to get there unnoticed. That was assuming there were none of their men guarding this side. There was at least a dozen of them around the main factory. She strained to listen for any signs but she was deafened by the sound of her own heart pumping in her head. What was she doing? Rafa was right. This was crazy. But all she could think of was Jair and then the photos of all the young boys killed by the army or the paramilitaries. She could not let that happen to her little brother.

She crept around the boat and started a brisk walk in the shadows of the mangroves. She was nearly halfway when the sound of another engine, or maybe two, became clear. She sank farther back into the mangroves and crouched down, peering through the foliage. Two cars – the same ones that had stopped her that time she met El Cubano – came around the corner and pulled up beside the General's car. Luzma's heart thumped louder. Car doors slammed, followed by footsteps. If these two men were meeting now, just hours after Jair was taken, the only way to find out what had happened to him was to follow them.

Luzma hurried to the corner where the two rivers met and the second factory jutted out into the water. The moon highlighted the river that was now at high tide and lapped the edge of the factory. How could she get in now? Then she heard a rustling behind her. She sank back into the mangroves, crouching down and holding her breath. Had they seen her? The noise grew louder. Where could she hide? Then she saw a glimpse of his wild curly black hair. Rafa. Thank God.

By the time they were at the edge of the second factory the water was up to Luzma's shoulders. Rafa was behind her, holding the small satchel that he carried everywhere with him, above his head. They ducked under the corner of the factory. Rafa clicked a button on his watch and a dull green light highlighted the wooden planks above their heads. He reached up and pushed the plank the kids had marked, it lifted up and he slid it to the side and light filtered down. Three more planks and there was a gap large enough to get through. Rafa pushed his bag through the gap and then hung on the edge and slowly pulled himself up, first just enough to look around and then his entire body. Then he reached down and held his hand down to Luzma.

Above them moonlight seeped in from slits in the corrugated iron roof. Luzma started to tiptoe towards the wall adjoining the other factory. The floorboards creaked under her feet. She froze. Then, reassured by the noises in the other factory: a mixture of music, voices and electrical equipment. Rafa and Luzma inched closer, squeezing through the stacks of timber on either side.

They reached the wall and looked through some of the smaller gaps in it, but all she could make out was the side of a grey metal structure. She looked up to where the boy had said Jair liked to hide. There was a flimsy staircase attached to the wall which led to a mezzanine level and there were several holes emitting bright light from the other room. She gingerly grasped the stairs and began to climb up, her legs shaking. The stairs groaned. She stopped, her ears tuned in to the adjoining wall. The mixture of sounds continued, but now the voices were getting louder, shouting. She was sure one of them belonged to the General. She continued up the stairs.

At the top she balanced on the narrow timber planks, sliding across to make room for Rafa. They looked through the holes in the wall, and then at each other. There was some sort of enormous steel vessel under construction, with half a dozen men working on it.

She pressed her face to the wall. Suddenly El Cubano stepped away from the side of the vessel and walked towards them, his face contorted. Her heartbeat accelerated. She glanced at Rafa. He was slowly reaching inside the bag slung over his shoulder removing his tiny Sony camcorder. He slipped the camera into his palm and pointed the small microphone forward and then pressed it into the gap in the wall he was looking through. Luzma's chest was tight. If the paramilitaries found them they would be killed on the spot.

'Don't come to my factory and talk about this in front of the men!' El Cubano shouted at the General as he stepped into view not far from them.

'Remember that you only have this factory as long as I let you stay here,' the General said. 'I will not lose my career over your stupid plan. Now did you bring the boy?'

Luzma sucked in a sharp breath. What were they going to do with him?

'No, I didn't bring him here. Don't be stupid. My men are dealing with him. Don't worry.'

Luzma could feel her heartbeat pounding in her head. It was so strong she had to strain to hear them. What did 'deal with him' mean?

'I need to talk to him. I need to know exactly what he heard and who he has told. That girl and the American came to the headquarters tonight asking for him, and threatening to get the US authorities involved as well as those people in the US who will bombard us with calls and make my life hell.'

'Well, did you arrest them or at least have them followed?'

'Arrest them for what? You want me to arrest a US citizen on no charges,' the General was pacing like a caged lion in front of El Cubano. 'I sent someone to follow them but he couldn't find them. He's gone to the American's house so we'll find them soon.'

'My men are very effective at getting information from people. We will find out everything the boy knows,' El Cubano said. 'And then we will get rid of him.'

Luzma fought the urge to vomit. She had to stop them. She would offer herself up in Jair's place. She moved slightly, readying herself to confront the two men. She glanced at Rafa who, as if reading her thoughts, shook his head slowly.

'No,' the General said, raising his hand. 'We might need him to get to the girl and the American. He stays alive until we have them and then you can do whatever you want with him.'

'And what if they've told the Americans or the national authorities?' El Cubano asked. 'They'll start swarming around this place. The plan will be destroyed and I will be a dead man.'

'If the Americans start calling asking about the boy or sending people down here then we need to make the boy disappear so no-one will ever find his remains. And we need to get rid of this whole operation,' the General said, pointing to the large vessel beside them.

'We cannot just get rid of this operation,' El Cubano said.

'It's worth hundreds of millions of dollars.'

'You had better hope you can find those two before they have the chance to tell the authorities. As long as they're walking around they're a threat to this operation. And if I hear any whispers that US or national authorities have been brought into it I am pulling the plug on this thing. You keep the boy alive and concentrate on getting the girl and the American.'

'You want them dead or alive?' El Cubano asked.

'You can do whatever you want with the girl, but with the American we have to make it seem like an accident or like the guerrilla did it.'

'How do you propose we do that?' El Cubano asked.

'I don't know yet, but find them, watch them, listen to their conversations and see who they're talking to,' the General said.

'We're going to have to get this thing in the water faster than planned,' El Cubano said. 'There's 100 million dollars' worth of merchandise waiting to be shipped and we've got to move it soon before this whole operation blows up.'

CHAPTER SIXTEEN

Every noise Luzma heard startled her as she and Rafa slowly edged their way back through the mangroves. Luzma's breathed in short, shallow breaths. All her senses were heightened. It seemed to take forever to get back to the car. The paramilitaries and the General wanted them dead; that was clear. Their lives were at a tipping point and there was no going back.

When they finally made it back to the car they both sat there staring at the factory, processing what they had just heard. Finally Rafa turned on the engine and started to slowly drive through the ghost-town streets. Luzma strained to see the road in front of them. She wound down the window a notch, listening. Were they footsteps she heard? 'Take the road to the left,' she whispered.

She wanted to see her family, to make sure they were all right, but Rafa said it was too dangerous, that the paramilitaries or the army would be watching Jolene's house. Luzma's chest constricted at the thought. Rafa said his boss, Claire, could help.

'Are you sure they won't also be guarding Claire's house?' she asked. 'It seems like they're looking for you as well.' Guilt washed over her. Rafa was in this mess because of her.

'We're not going to her house; we're going to her boyfriend's place. It's closer and I'm sure she'll be there.'

Suddenly Rafa hit the brakes as a tall figure that stepped in front of them. Luzma sucked the night's cold air and sat rigid. The man stood still before them and then slowly turned and crossed the road. Rafa and Luzma exhaled deeply, relieved. It was just a man crossing the road.

Rafa pulled the car into a small alleyway. Luzma's body was thrust from side to side as the vehicle navigated the uneven, muddy road. Rafa slid the car into an empty lot between two small homes. Luzma stepped out and felt heavy under the weight of her tensed muscles and sweat-dampened clothes. The mud squelched beneath her feet as they walked back along the side of the alleyway. They scanned the road then quickly ran across.

After ten minutes Luzma was sure they were walking in a circle but didn't dare break the silence to ask. Rafa led her down a small pathway between rows of homes. Rafa stopped at the doorway at the back of one of the homes. He tried the handle, but it was locked. They went to the side of the house and knocked on a window, a low insistent tap. Profanities emanated out of the darkness then a curtain was wrenched back and a light shone in their face.

'Rafa, what the hell are you doing?' a male voice said. 'It's not even light.'

'Let us in.'

Josu, one of the Afro-Colombian rights leaders who'd been introduced to her at the first victim's gathering she attended with Rafa, opened the back door, a towel wrapped around his waist. 'Brother, what the hell is going on?'

Rafa locked the door behind them. 'We're in serious trouble. We need your help.'

A woman entered the room. Her skin appeared translucent under the dull light bulb that flickered to life above their heads, her curly orange hair, untamed. She rubbed her eyes and looked at them in a daze.

'Rafa, you look like you're in trouble!' she said. 'Hi, I'm Claire,' she said to Luzma. 'I'll get you some clean clothes, you can wash off and then tell us what's going on.'

'You followed the General and El Cubano to the factory?' Claire asked, incredulously after Luzma finished telling the story about Jair's kidnapping and meeting the General. 'Are you trying to get yourself killed?'

'It gets worse,' Rafa said.

'Well, I need a cigarette before I hear any more,' Claire said, her sinewy white body slipping out of the room. She came back moments later and leaned against the kitchen bench, cigarette in one hand, her other arm folded across her chest. The flickering light of the cigarette highlighted the crease that ran between her eyes up to her forehead. It seemed to deepen the more they spoke. 'So, how does it get worse?'

'Several weeks ago we were shown a secret entrance into the adjoining factory where you can see everything in the main factory that the paramilitaries are using. Tonight we used that to get in and listen to them.' Rafa hesitated, shaking his head. 'Claire, they're up to something big.'

The room was silent apart from the crackle of Claire's cigarette as she inhaled.

'They're building an enormous vessel. It looks like a submarine,' Rafa said. 'They have a whole team of people working on it. When Jair heard them talking about needing to kill some community leaders, the General specifically said it was because they were snooping around the factory and it could cost them millions of dollars. We heard the same thing tonight.'

'A submarine!' Josu exclaimed. 'It would explain why they needed the factory and why they took over San Francisco and have been killing so many people.'

'They're going to kill many more, including my brother if we don't stop them,' Luzma said.

Claire sucked on her cigarette. 'We have to call our contacts in the US and get them to bombard the national and local authorities with calls about your brother's kidnapping. That usually works.'

'No, I thought that too when Jair was first kidnapped.' Luzma said, another wave of panic and concern rising inside of her. 'If you do that they'll kill him. We heard the General say to El Cubano that if they hear anything from the Americans or the national authorities they had to kill Jair and would make sure he was never found.'

'These men are extremely dangerous. El Cubano will kill you simply because you looked at him the wrong way. But if you stand in the way of him and what he cares most about, money, well.' Josu ran a finger across his throat.

'And the General isn't much better,' Rafa added. 'You've heard what he and his men have done to innocent civilians.'

Fury curdled in Luzma's gut. She would not let Jair die. And she would not be cowed by these men. Now, more than ever, she wanted justice. She had lost her mother and her family had been forced to leave their home. Enough was enough. Desperate ideas dashed through her mind and she grabbed at whatever she could. 'I could offer them a swap: Jair for me and then once he is free tell your contacts to do whatever they can to stop these animals.'

'That's suicide and you know it,' Rafa said. 'They'll kill Jair as soon as they have you. The best thing you can do for him is to stay alive.'

Outside the window the light was changing as the sun came up. How many days were left before they killed Jair? 'I need to rescue my brother. I promised to protect him. Can't someone, anyone help get him back?' Luzma asked, her voice breaking with emotion.

'We can't ask the army or the police, that's clear. The normal registry for missing people is run through the local government and they have proven they are not trustworthy,' Claire said. 'The reality is that the Americans are not going to send a search party.'

'But they would be very interested to know what the paramilitaries are doing in the factory,' Rafa said. 'It will have something to do with drugs destined for the US.'

'Yes, they would be interested in proving that El Cubano and the General were jointly running this operation. But what's that got to do with the boy?' Claire asked.

'We have proof now that El Cubano and the General are involved. That, and footage of the vessel are two things the US government would be very interested in,' Rafa said, slowly and carefully.

'What footage do you have?' Josu asked.

'I taped the conversation between the General and El Cubano on my camera when we were inside the factory. I can download it to your computer.'

'Jesus, Rafa, what the hell have you got yourself into?' Claire exclaimed. She pulled out another cigarette and hurriedly lit it. 'I don't like where you're going with this.'

'We could threaten the General with the recording – either he returns Jair or we send it to the authorities,' Luzma said. 'Or we can share it directly with the US authorities and say in return we want their help to figure out where Jair is.'

'The first idea will get you killed and the second is a bloody long shot,' Claire said.

'Do you have any better ideas?' Luzma said. She didn't have time to be presented with the problems. She needed a solution fast.

'The US authorities are definitely going to want the information we have so they might be willing to offer us some sort of help in return,' Rafa said. 'I'm not saying they're going to rescue Jair, but they might just be able to provide us some information that could help us get to Jair.'

'Rafa, I understand you want to help but the people who would be interested in this information are the US Drug Enforcement Administration, maybe the CIA,' Claire said. 'The Drug Enforcement Administration has the sole mission of fighting drugs, not rescuing kids who have been kidnapped.'

'I'm sorry but I'm leaving. I'm not going to lose any more time talking about this,' Luzma said, determinedly as she stood up. 'I will save my brother even if it gets me killed. But this isn't just about him. They can't keep on getting away with this with no consequences. Ten people have been killed in the past couple of weeks just in San Francisco and hundreds have been killed in the past year. Several dozen have been murdered for no reason by the armed forces in Buenaventura last year. Girls' dismembered bodies have been hung up in town. So many of us have been victims in some way and what happens to them? Absolutely nothing.'

'Luzma's right,' Rafa said. 'We've been denouncing paramilitary and army killings and torture here for years and what's changed? The General is still in place. The paramilitaries are brutal as ever. The official statistics of killings may have dropped slightly but that's because now they take more care to get rid of the bodies. If you don't have a body you don't count as an official murder.'

Rafa paused and exhaled with frustration. 'If the thing they care most about is money, and they apparently have a lot of money on the line at the moment, then we have to target their weak spot. With this video we have the proof that we need to get the General and El Cubano behind bars where they belong.'

'So are you suggesting that the DEA is going to help rescue Luzma's brother?' Claire asked, her voice soft but still doubtful.

Rafa leaned back, looking at the ceiling as if searching for inspiration. 'I don't know yet. But, as I said, I'm sure they'll want this information and hopefully in return they can help us in some way. I know that's not a lot to go on, but it's the only suggestion I have.'

'In that case we will do what we can to help you,' she said.

'How do we contact them?' Luzma asked Rafa.

'I have a friend.'

Luzma sat in the sparse cement kitchen alone. She glanced down the hallway, wondering how Rafa's call to his contact in the US Embassy was going. Claire and Josu were in another room downloading the recording Rafa had made at the factory last night. Luzma longed to be with Jair, Grandma and Grandpa and all their neighbors in Las Delicias in the kitchen filled with herbs and potions, the sounds of laughter, music and the hiss of frying plantains filling the room, the smell of coconut and cilantro wafting through the air. A blanket of loneliness smothered her.

She stared Rafa's open satchel and saw his phone. He had told her that they would call Grandma and Grandpa later. But she desperately needed to hear their voices and make sure that they were all right. She dialled Aunt Jolene's number.

'Hello.' Aunty's voice was strained.

'It's Luzma. Is everybody there okay?'

'*Ah Santa Maria Purisimo*, thank God you're okay,' Jolene said.

In the background she could hear Grandpa and Grandma's voices. Luzma forced back the tears that were welling in her eyes. She did not want her family to worry about her. She had to be strong for them.

'Luzma, are you okay? Where are you? Do you know anything about Jair?' Jolene frantically fired questions at her.

Luzma felt a lump in her throat at the mention of her brother's name. 'Jair is...' Suddenly the phone was snatched from her hand.

Rafa was beside her and Claire and Josu stood in the doorway.

'Luzma, what are you doing?' Rafa hissed. 'As far as we know they might have your aunt's phone tapped.' He lifted his hand and put the phone to his ear. 'Hi, it's Rafa. I'm sorry it's just that I'm worried about using the phone. I think you'll understand,' he said into the mouthpiece, his jaw tight. 'Yes, don't worry. I'll look after her.' He handed her back the phone.

'One minute and don't mention anything you've seen or where we are.'

Luzma stared at him, shocked by his coldness.

'Luzma, are you okay, my love?' Grandma asked. Her voice sounded more like a child than the powerful woman Luzma had known all her life.

'Yes, I'm fine. I love you so much. Please be careful.'

'No, *mi hijita*, you be careful. May God and the Orisha protect you and Jair,' she said.

'Tell Grandpa I promise I'll find Jair.'

'Luzma, don't do anything stupid. Take care.'

'You have got to get out of Buenaventura as soon as possible,' Claire said after watching the footage Rafa had filmed in the factory. 'You heard them. They want to kill you.'

Josu looked at Rafa. 'Brother, you've been here for three years now. You know what they're like. If they want you dead your days are numbered.'

Suddenly there was a knock. Luzma's gaze darted to the door. They waited, ears trained. Rafa reached slowly for his camera, unplugged it and put it back in his bag. Claire saved the recording and was shutting down the computer. The banging returned, only louder, more insistent. Claire, Rafa and Josu exchanged glances.

'It's them, isn't it?' Luzma whispered.

Claire stood and slid down the hallway. Josu motioned for Luzma and Rafa to stay as he made his way to the back door. Luzma looked down the hallway, where Claire was delicately peeling back the curtain to look out. She recoiled, spun around and returned mouthing the word 'army'.

They were there. Had they followed them or was it the phone call Luzma had made? What would they do with them? They needed to get out of there. Josu came back and motioned to the back door and mouthed the very same word. They had both exits covered. There was no way out. The knocking grew louder and faster.

'Josu Mosquera, please open the door. This is Colonel Perez from the Armed Forces.'

If the army found them they would be killed. They had to run or hide and they needed to do it fast because the hammering on the door was growing more insistent. They were going to come in whether invited or not. Luzma grabbed Josu's hand.

'Where can we hide?'

He looked around and then stood, motioning for them to follow him into the bedroom. 'Claire, you answer the door, distract them,' he whispered

There didn't seem anywhere to hide in the tiny room apart from under the bed and surely that would be futile. But he pointed to a cupboard high up in the corner, above Luzma's head. He bent his leg and motioned for Rafa to use it to step on to hoist himself up.

'Can I help you?' Claire's voice echoed down the hallway.

'Is the owner of this property, Josu Mosquera, here?' a male voice responded.

Luzma silently urged Rafa to hurry as he shuffled backwards into the small cupboard, his body hunching and twisting to fit into the space.

'Yes, he's in bed. He had a late night. Can I help you with something?'

Josu gave Luzma a hand and she stepped on his leg and pulled herself up with Rafa's help.

'Honey, who is it?' Josu called out, feigning a dazed voice.

Luzma shuffled around until her back was pressed against the wall and her body huddled into Rafa's. They slid the door shut.

'It's the Army. They want to speak to you,' Claire called back.

Luzma and Rafa were enclosed in darkness apart from a few cracks of light at the edges of the cupboard door. Luzma's sense of sound became more attuned. She could hear Josu's bare feet treading against the floorboards leading to the front; someone in the alleyway whispering.

'I'm Josu. What do you want?' His voice was tinged with irritation.

'We're looking for a friend of yours, Rafael Wilson, and we believe he may be here.'

Luzma's head was propped awkwardly on Rafa's shoulder and close enough to hear his rapid heartbeat. How had she managed to get him in so much trouble?

'I know Rafael, but he's not here. Why are you looking for him?' Josu said.

'Let us in so we can discuss this in private,' the voice said.

Luzma shifted, straining to hear what was being said. The wood underneath her groaned with their weight. She froze. Rafa's heartbeat accelerated. Silence.

'Fine, you can come in,' Josu said.

Multiple footsteps moved in their direction. Luzma tried to make out how many people were inside the house. She imagined there must be at least two of them, plus Claire and Josu. Somewhere in the alleyway in front of them there was a slight rustle. There must be more of them outside circling the house. What would they do if they captured them?

'Do you mind if we look around?' It sounded more like an order than a question.

'Do you have a warrant?' Claire's voice sounded high-pitched and strained, her accent thicker than normal. 'You can't come in here without a warrant.'

'Sorry. What was your name?' The man's voice was polite, but there was an undertone of threat.

'Claire Wellington. I'm an Australian citizen. I'm the local director of Peace Brigades International. I know my rights.'

As she spoke footsteps slowly moved closer. Luzma's heart beat faster and louder.

'Ms Wellington, we are just trying to help your friend and colleague, Rafael Wilson. We believe he may be in grave danger.'

Grave danger? They were the ones who wanted him dead.

'What are you talking about?' Claire asked.

The sound of feet shuffling towards them grew louder.

'We have gathered intelligence information that Luz-Marina Cuesta has become a target of the FARC guerrilla because of her and her brother's ties to the paramilitaries. Mr Wilson is in danger by association. Because he is a US citizen we want to try to help him before the guerrilla get to them.'

Fury surged inside of Luzma. She felt like shouting at them that the only association she had with the paramilitaries was that they'd kidnapped her brother and it was the army who had the ties.

'Hey, what are you doing?' Josu's shouted. 'You can't just come in and walk around my house as you please.'

The footsteps sounded as if they were just beside Luzma, but were probably at the entrance to the bedroom and then stepping into the room. They were followed by four loud thuds.

'If you want to look through my house you should go get a warrant,' Josu said. His voice was close, he was now in the room as well.

'Do you have something to hide, Mr Mosquerra?'

'No, but would you like people barging into your house like this at this hour?'

The movement was directly in front of the cupboard. Could he hear Luzma breathing? She tried to slow it down, but it only came out faster and shallower, with a slight rasp. *God, Orishas, please make them go away.*

More footsteps.

'What's your name?' Claire asked, imperiously.

'Colonel Perez.'

'Well, Colonel Perez, thank you for telling us about Rafael. I find that very concerning. I will contact him immediately and my boss in the United States to inform them. We don't have any more information for you. As you can see we are by ourselves. If you want to look through our house you will have to come back with a warrant because otherwise I will have to report you to the national authorities and I don't think you want that.'

In the silence that followed Luzma willed herself to be still. In the small, cramped space the sound of her breath seemed amplified.

'We will be back shortly.' The footsteps retreated.

How long did she and Rafa have before they would return and search the house? They would find them for sure. How could they possibly escape if the army was patrolling the perimeter?

CHAPTER SEVENTEEN

General Ordonez sat in his director's chair in his large sterile office. The early morning light fell across the wall in front of him, highlighting the meticulously organized rows of framed awards. They boasted a highly successful twenty-four-year military career. But that could all be in jeopardy if that girl and her American friend started speaking in Bogota or internationally about the conversation the boy had overheard. Right now, the head of the army was congratulating him for having one of the best combat kill rates in the country and for ousting the guerrilla from San Francisco. He had hinted that Ordonez would be in line for a promotion if he kept up the good work. But if calls started coming from Washington claiming multiple civilian killings in the operation to take over San Francisco, or open collusion with the paramilitaries, the army would have to investigate. And if they came right now they would find a factory guarded by paramilitary troops with a professional submarine inside. He would be hauled off to America on drug trafficking charges.

Ordonez's head pounded at the thought. Why had he got involved with this plan? It was one thing to collude with the paramilitaries to help oust the guerrilla. Most of his colleagues did that. Getting involved in trafficking was a different story. How could he have resisted that money? With just one shipment he could get himself a condo in Bogota, a holiday house in San Andres and lots of diamonds to impress his hard-to-please lover. That was the life he deserved. He had dedicated years of his life to fighting for his country, half of that in the humid jungle being eaten alive by insects and leeches. Instead of getting the post he wanted in Medellin, he had been sent to Buenaventura, a smelly hellhole without culture and full of *Negros*. He needed to get the job done as fast as possible and get good money for the sacrifices he had made.

The phone rang. Ordonez straightened. It was Colonel Perez, who he had sent to find the girl and the American.

'Do you have them?'

'No, sir,' the Colonel said. 'The call was traced to a house in barrio Yeres belonging to Josu Mosquera who is one of the leaders of the organization that is always carrying on about Afro-Colombian rights and all that crap. We did a preliminary search of the house but couldn't find them inside or anywhere in the area. We couldn't do a thorough search as they demanded we show them a warrant.'

The General slammed his fist into the desk. 'A warrant? Who does he think he is? Get back inside and search every inch of that house.'

'Yes, sir. It's just that there's a complication,' the Colonel said softly.

'You mean apart from the fact that you lost the girl even though we had her location?' the General said through gritted teeth.

'Sir, Josu is not alone. He's with Claire Wellington. She's an Australian citizen working with the American and is the local leader of Peace Brigades International.'

The General further clenched his fist, as if he was ready to throw a punch. The last thing he needed was another foreigner mixed up in this. If they kept it local he could control it, but he did not want international attention at the moment. 'What have you told her so far?'

'Just that we were looking for Luz-Marina Cuesta and Rafael Wilson as we have intel that they've become a target of the guerrillas due to Ms Cuesta and her brother's association with the paramilitaries,' the Colonel said. 'I said we were just trying to protect them.'

'Good work, Colonel. Stay with them until I call you. I'll get you a warrant to search the place and I'm sending undercover agents to follow Claire and Josu. Hopefully they'll lead us back to the girl and the American.'

The General hung up the phone and exhaled slowly, staring at the solitary photo that sat on his desk. His father, then Commander-in-Chief of the Armed Forces, stood tall and proud beside him the day he entered the armed forces. He could remember his father's words before he left for the department of Putumayo to begin his career in the army.

'You have to be willing to do whatever it takes to achieve your objective. Never pay attention to your emotions. You decide what you need to do and then you act. You kill the enemy, and every last one of their friends because if you don't, they will kill you. There is no option. They die or you die.'

That was the last time he had seen his father. The guerrillas attacked the family farm and managed to kill all the guards and his father as well. There were no survivors from that attack twenty-three years ago, but General Ordonez was sure his father had gone down fighting.

He picked up his phone and dialed.

Marcos Menendez, the regional director of the SIJIN, the army's intelligence agency, was a short stocky man. As he stood to attention before General Ordonez he had to crane his neck to look up at his superior.

'General, they said you needed to see me,' he said in the thick accent of the *Paises* from Medellin.

'Yes, I need intel on two people,' the General said, passing Menendez a piece of paper.

'Luz-Marina Cuesta and Rafael Wilson,' Menendez read. 'Wilson is an unusual surname. Where is he from?'

'The United States.'

Menendez raised an eyebrow. 'Is this joint intel with the CIA or is this off the radar?'

'Strictly off the radar. I don't want the CIA or anyone else in the US Embassy involved or made aware of in any way. These two are those human rights types that help the guerrilla. They're not happy that we're making so much progress so they are creating problems for us.'

Menendez simply nodded. 'I understand, sir. What type of intel do you need exactly?'

'I want to know all of their friends, family and colleagues and I want every single one of their phones tapped. These two have gone missing and have become a liability. If you find their location I want to know immediately. I also want to know anything that any of their contacts say that might be of interest to us.'

'Yes, sir. I will do that. Anything else?'

'Maybe you could explore options to, how should I say, put in question their legitimacy.' The General's words were slow and measured.

'Like proof of links to the guerrilla or maybe drug trafficking?' Menendez asked.

The General simply nodded.

CHAPTER EIGHTEEN

Guaviare, Colombia

'Hit them with the M-60!' US Drug Enforcement Administration Andean Director, Chuck Harrison exclaimed as bullets narrowly missed the Colombian national police helicopter.

Around a dozen FARC soldiers guarded the jungle laboratory below them. Armed with AK-47s they fired relentlessly on the chopper. There was a loud twang as a bullet hit the tail and the helicopter swerved to the side.

'What's the damage?' Chuck asked the pilot in front of him.

'They missed the engine. We're fine.'

'You need to take them out before they get a better aim.'

The officer beside Chuck pointed the M-60 machine gun at the laboratory and opened fire. The other police helicopter began to barrage the guerrilla with bullets from the other side. At least half of the FARC soldiers were down and the others fled into the jungle.

'Time to go in on foot,' Chuck said. 'Keep the other helicopter in the air.'

The pilot hovered over a small clearing and two ropes were dropped from the side of the helicopter. Chuck followed his colleagues in the Elite National Police and Narcotics squad as they repelled to the ground.

Dressed in a bulletproof vest and helmet and carrying his Glock model 1, Chuck and his seven colleagues worked their way through the thick jungle.

The laboratory was a crudely constructed timber building with an outside covered area. Underneath were rows of industrial-sized metal drums with coca leaves soaking in gasoline and other chemicals. To the side of the building several large generators hummed loudly.

The squad commander pointed to his men to surround the building while he and Chuck went inside.

Vats lined the far wall. The first had the acidic smell of acetone, while water was still boiling in others, ready for the crystallisation process. Cartons of methyl ethyl ketone and hydrochloric acid were lined up on the adjacent bench. There were around two dozen microwaves around the room and the middle counter looked like a science lab.

Chuck pulled back a tarpaulin in the far corner revealing bricks of cocaine, lined up ready to be transported.

'How much is there?' the commander asked.

'About 1000 kilos I'd say,' Chuck said, adding. 'That's worth about thirty million dollars wholesale in the US. This is quite a busy operation.'

'I'll collect a sample to send to our lab in DC,' he said. 'You get your men to take an inventory of all the gear.'

The commander left the room and came back with two police officers who began to photograph and document everything. They collected the handful of radios, a cell phone and a laptop. Hopefully some useful evidence.

'Let's torch this place,' Chuck said, once the inventory had been finished and all evidence collected.

His satellite phone rang.

'Hello.'

'Chuck, it's Cheryl,' his personal secretary said.

'I'm a little busy right now,' Chuck said, watching the police wire explosives up around the building and all the equipment.

'Sorry, but Jeff from the political section said it was important. He said he has information about Buenaventura that might interest you and wants to meet ASAP.'

'I'll be back in Bogota this afternoon. Set up a meeting.'

US Embassy, Bogota, Colombia

As soon as Jeff Brighton left his office Chuck called Nathaniel Davidson, the head of the Cali regional office.

'Nat, how quickly can you get to Buenaventura?'

'I can be there in the morning, sir,' Nathaniel said. 'What do you have?'

Chuck couldn't believe that after five years working together the former marine still called him sir. It made Chuck feel older than his fifty years.

'I need you to meet with an American by the name of Rafael Wilson and his Colombian girlfriend, Luz-Marina Cuesta,' he said. 'It seems they may have some very interesting information, including a video, on the elusive Pablo Ruiz.'

'What sort of information?' Nathaniel asked.

'It's best you talk to them and then let me know,' Chuck said.

'Jeff's giving them your numbers so expect a call. And, Nat, get on it quickly. It sounds like they've made it onto Ruiz's hit list so we need to get to them before he does.'

'Got it. I'll get back to you as soon as we've had the meeting.'

After hanging up Chuck looked at the large organigram of the Norte de Valle Cartel on his computer. Chuck had hoped they would be closer by now, especially after intercepting the cartel's shipment of 1000 kilos of cocaine into Miami and arresting two of the cartel's top men in the US nearly nine months ago. But one of them had already been killed in prison and the other was too afraid to talk. Fernando Guitterez had an uncanny ability to make evidence and people disappear, earning him the name 'El Magico'. Pablo Ruiz was on the third row down and believed to be in charge of Guitterez's Pacific operations. But, they had not been able to tie him to anything. Yet. *Could this video be the intel they had been looking for?*

Guitterrez was an ambitious son of a bitch. He seemed to be determined to oust the Mexicans from the equation and return his cartel to the glory days where the Colombians were the undisputed Kings of Cocaine, swamping the US market. Chuck couldn't let that happen. Not on his watch.

CHAPTER NINETEEN

Luzma rested her head on the bars covering the window, the metal cold against her forehead. The long winding driveway that led up to the nun's retreat centre was empty. They should have been there half an hour ago. When Rafa had called the DEA agent he had said 5.30pm.

Luzma was grateful that Josu's plan for them to escape with the help of his neighbor had worked and that Sister Clara had agreed to hide them. But all she could think about was Jair. The more time that passed the greater risk he was in.

They heard a car engine nearby and then a large black truck appeared in the driveway.

'They're here,' she announced.

The driver's door opened. A black man stood up stiffly as if he struggled against the weight of his large muscular body. The man on the other side of the vehicle seemed childlike in comparison. Sister Clara came out the front to greet the men and then led them inside. Luzma pulled up a table and four chairs and waited.

The door clicked open and Sister Clara walked in with the hulk-like man looming over her and the other behind. Even Rafa had to crane his head to look up at the man as he stepped in front of him and held out his hand.

'I'm Nathaniel Davidson from the US Drug Enforcement Administration,' he addressed Rafa and then turned to shake

Luzma's hand. He spoke Spanish with an even more marked drawl than Rafa.

'I'm Jose Guevara also with the DEA,' the other man said, his tone and attitude more relaxed than his partner.

'Why don't you all have a seat and I'll leave you to talk,' Sister Clara said, letting herself out.

'Did Jeff tell you about what happened to Luzma's brother, Jair?' Rafa asked.

The large man nodded. 'Yes, he said he'd been taken by unidentified armed men and you believe that the army and the paramilitaries are involved and that you are both targets.'

The matter-of-fact way he described the situation irritated Luzma. This was her brother, not a statistic on a report.

As if picking up on her thoughts the other man said, 'We're sorry about what's happened to your brother. We understand you must be very concerned."

'We were also told that you were able to get inside the factory in San Francisco and have some information that could be very useful to our operation,' Nathaniel Davidson said.

'Yes, that's true,' Luzma said. 'But first we'd like to know how you might be able to help us get my brother back safely.'

'From what we heard last night,' Rafa added, 'it's not safe for us to go through the normal channels of domestic and international advocacy.'

The two men glanced at each other and then Nathanial nodded to his colleague.

'You have to realize that we have a very specific role to investigate and ultimately dismantle and bring to justice the drug cartels,' Jose said. 'As you can imagine, it's a role that takes up a lot of time and resources. But, a very important job, especially in a country like Colombia. We are focused solely on that objective so we pass other issues, such as kidnappings and human rights abuses, to our colleagues in other sections of the embassy.'

'We can't talk to the political section,' Luzma said. 'If we play you the video, you will see that El Cubano and General Ordonez explicitly said that if they get any sense that the national or international authorities have been alerted, they'll kill Jair. They're only keeping him alive until they can catch us.'

'I have very close contacts with the staff in the political division and am in regular contact with them,' Rafa said. 'But as Luzma explained, we can't go down that route this time.'

'It's far too dangerous for you two to stay in Buenaventura,' Nathaniel said. 'We can get you out safely.'

Luzma cut him off. 'I am not leaving Buenaventura. Not until I have my brother with me. We want to know if you have any information that might help us locate Jair or know how to get him back.'

Rafa took Luzma's hand and looked at her. 'Luzma, they're right. It's far too dangerous for us in Buenaventura. If the paramilitaries and the General want us killed, we won't survive here for long.'

'I think you're right. You should leave. But I can't. I'll stay here until I get Jair back.'

'The only thing keeping Jair alive right now is the fact that they haven't caught you yet,' Rafa said. 'If you stay here, they'll find you.'

'Rafa, the only home I have is my family and the most important part of that has been taken. I won't leave until I have him. My gut instinct is that if I leave he will be killed. I don't know how to get him back, but I'll find a way.'

Rafa sighed and looked at the two men staring silently at him.

'I'm not leaving her here alone, so it looks like we're staying.'

'That's not advisable and you know it,' Nathanial said.

Luzma was torn. She was relieved that Rafa had offered to stay with her and she wouldn't be alone but if Rafa got hurt, or worse, she would never forgive herself. 'I want you to stay, but I know you should leave. This is something I have to deal with. You shouldn't put your life at risk for me.'

'I'm not going to lose someone else I care about. If you're staying, so am I,' he said and then turned to the US agents. 'We're both staying in Buenaventura. We do have a video that would be of interest to you. So, are you able to help us in any way?'

There was silence for a moment while the agents glanced at each other.

'I'm going to be straight with you,' Nathaniel said. 'Our possibilities are limited. Depending on what you show us, we may open an operation here and there's a distant possibility that we might find out something about the boy, in which case we will share it with you. If you change your mind, which I would urge you to, we can get you out of Buenaventura safely.'

'If you have evidence that would help us link El Cubano and General Ordonez to drug trafficking operations, then we need to look at it,' Jose said. 'I'm sure you want them brought to justice and this evidence might help us do that.'

'I want them both to rot in jail,' Luzma said. 'But first I want Jair back, so please help us any way you can.'

'Deal,' Nathanial said, nodding.

'Do you have a laptop or should we watch the footage on the camera?' Rafa asked, pulling out his small camcorder.

Jose Guevara pulled out a small laptop from his bag and placed it on the table. Rafa plugged in his camera and fiddled around until the image came up on the screen. He swivelled the computer around and pressed play.

The two men moved closer, focusing intently on the screen.

'You thinking the same thing I am?' Jose said, glancing at his colleague.

Nathanial simply nodded, leaning in closer to the screen. The light from the screen played across his face, highlighting the tightening of the muscles around his eyes.

When the footage finally ended they all sat in silence, with the two men continuing to stare at the screen. Luzma and Rafa watched them, waiting.

'Thank you, this is far more useful than we could have possibly imagined,' Jose said. 'Do you mind if we copy it?'

'Sure,' Rafa said.

'I hope that you realize this isn't just about drugs,' Luzma said. 'These two men are responsible for the killing, disappearance and torture of many innocent people.'

'Yes, but the drug trade is one of the main motivators behind all that violence,' Nathanial said. 'How did you get inside the factory? It would be heavily guarded'

'There's not much security around the adjoining factory. It's stacked high with timber waiting to be shipped. Some of the local kids showed us a way to get inside from the outer corner near the mangroves and once you're inside there are spots where you can see into the main factory.'

'What made you think to record what you were seeing?' Nathaniel asked.

Rafa shrugged. 'I make documentaries. If I see something's not quite right, something I believe needs attention, I will naturally make a recording.'

'It was very brave of you both to have gone in there and to have gathered this evidence,' Jose said, closing his computer and putting it back in his bag. 'It will be very useful for us.'

'It would also be very helpful to know someone on the inside with access to the main factory. Do you know anyone?'

'We don't tend to hang out with paramilitaries,' Luzma said curtly. But then a thought came to her: What about Diana's boyfriend Mauricio? Diana said he had been recruited by the General for a project inside the factory.

'I do know of someone. He is an electrician in the army but has recently been recruited to work in the factory.'

'Do you think he would talk to us? Is he supportive of the paramilitaries?'

'His girlfriend said he wants to get out of the army because he hates the things he sees them do, but he's too scared for his safety and he needs the money to take care of his family in Cali. Since he has been recruited to work in the factory, he is even more fearful and won't talk to anyone, not even his girlfriend, about what's going on there.'

'Luzma, we want these criminals in jail, just like you. If you can find us someone on the inside you could help us do that,' Nathaniel said.

CHAPTER TWENTY

Luzma felt as if everyone was watching them as she and Rafa walked the block from where they'd parked Sister Clara's car to Mauricio's house, where they were meeting Diana. A fisherman who sat beside the dirt road repairing his net paused to watch them pass. Young kids running around after each other stopped to stare. In Buenaventura you couldn't trust anyone.

Rafa and Diana were in danger just being with her. Diana had suggested they meet in Mauricio's home in case hers was being watched. But who was to say they hadn't been followed, despite all the precautions they'd taken. It seemed like trouble followed Luzma.

Diana opened the door and gasped when she saw Luzma. 'Have you spoken to your grandparents?'

'What's wrong?' Luzma asked, horrible possibilities flooding her mind.

'The paramilitaries went to the house to talk to them,' Diana said.

Fear began to squeeze Luzma's chest and her breath became shallow. 'Are they all right? Please tell me they're safe?'

'They're all right,' Diana said.

'What did the paramilitaries tell them?'

Diana looked away and let out a sigh, her chest sinking.

Luzma reached across and grabbed her arm. 'Diana, please tell me what they said.'

'The paras told them they had to convince you to go to El Cubano before Friday.'

'Or what?' Luzma asked, barely able to speak.

'They said if you didn't meet with El Cubano by Friday they would start killing your family, one by one.'

Luzma felt as if she had been hit with a heavy weight. She stood and walked, dizzy and disoriented, in a daze towards the door. There was only one thing she could think of doing to put a stop to all of this madness.

'What are you doing?' Diana and Rafa's voices mingled together.

'I'm going to see El Cubano,' she replied, reaching for the door handle.

Rafa's hand encircled hers and pulled it away. He turned her around to face him. 'Luzma, he will rape, torture and kill you.'

'Yes, but if I don't go he'll kill my family.'

Rafa gripped her shoulders. 'Please just sit down and we'll figure something out.'

'This is my fault,' Luzma said. 'I have to protect my family, even if it gets me killed.' *How the hell were people meant to fight against these men when they had the arms, the power, the money and the connections to do whatever the hell they wanted to?*

Diana sighed and sank down on a plastic chair below a tattered poster of God looking down at Mary and baby Jesus. A tunnel of light from a gap in the wall shone across her hands. 'I know what it's like to feel guilty,' she said. 'I spent so much time thinking everything that happened was my fault. I blamed myself when they killed my first boyfriend and dad and even for the stuff they did to me.'

Her words brought back the other memory that Luzma always tried so hard to squash. 'My dad always blamed me for Mum's death,' she said, looking at the dirty floor. 'He said if I hadn't told her that the paramilitary officer had raped me, she would never have gone to confront the leader.'

'Oh, Luzma,' Rafa gently stroked her back.

Luzma shrugged. The niggling feeling of guilt never really went away and she had spent her life pushing it down, always making up for her so-called sin. Shifting tack, as now wasn't the time to dwell on the past, Luzma continued. 'We can't waste any time. We need to figure out how to secure my family's safety.'

Luzma wanted to stop El Cubano and General Ordonez and the others involved from hurting anyone else. But right now, Jair and her family were her priority. 'We need to get my family out of here somehow,' she said.

'The problem is that the paras are watching Jolene's house and they're probably following them,' Diana said. It was midday and the tin roof in Mauricio's tiny home transferred the heat, making the air stifling. Luzma wiped the sweat off her brow.

'The US government officials said they could help us get out of Buenaventura,' she said to Rafa. 'Why don't we ask them to help my family instead?'

'Maybe. We can ask,' Rafa said. 'Or we can talk to Jhon Jairo who works at the docks. He loads the trucks and is friends with lots of drivers so maybe he could think of a way to sneak them out on one of the trucks headed for Bogota or Medellin every day.'

'Are you two going to leave with them?' Diana asked.

'No,' Luzma replied. 'I was hoping you could help me, Diana.'

'Of course, I want to help, but I don't really know what use I can be.'

Luzma explained to her about the conversation with the US DEA and about how they needed someone inside the factory to help them.

Diana stiffened. 'You want Mauricio to help them, don't you?' she asked, her voice expressionless

Luzma shifted, uncomfortable asking for something that would put Mauricio in danger. But if it might help Jair she had to do it. The agents had said they could help Mauricio.

'You've told me how unhappy he is in the army and how he wants to escape, especially now, but he feels trapped.' Luzma fidgeted as she spoke.

'Yes, but I've also told you how afraid he is to be working in the factory and how tight the security is.' Diana's voice was now sharp and brittle.

Luzma winced, sad that she had angered Diana.

'I'm sorry,' Diana said. 'It's just that I really love Mauricio and I can't bear the thought of losing someone else I love.'

She knew how Diana felt and she didn't want to risk putting her in that position. She tried to justify it to herself. This might be his only chance of escaping. 'I totally understand. But the US agents said they would help Mauricio. This could be his way to escape and yours too.' As she spoke she tried to convince herself that she really was trying to help Mauricio. But in reality she was only thinking of herself and Jair. She was ashamed to be so selfish.

Diana stared at her. Luzma was sure the woman could see through her and her motives. She looked down to avoid Diana's gaze.

'Do you really think they'd help him? Don't you think it could be dangerous?'

Luzma shrugged again. She didn't really know and she could not bring herself to lie, no matter how much she wanted her help. 'Maybe he could speak to them himself and see what they say. I don't think there's any harm in doing that.'

'Okay, I'll tell him and suggest he talks to them,' Diana said slowly. 'How would he get in contact with them?'

Luzma pulled out the two business cards the agents had given her and wrote down their information. She couldn't bear to think of what could happen to her family and now to Diana's as well.

CHAPTER TWENTY-ONE

It was called the dungeon. A sterile, windowless room with soundproof walls, the most secure meeting area in the US Embassy in Bogota. It always gave Chuck a sense of claustrophobia. He poured himself his fourth cup of coffee for the day. He had barely slept for the past week since seeing the video Nathaniel had brought back from Buenaventura. An enlarged image of the submarine that was caught in the video was now sitting in front of him and the other three men in the room: Sean Perry, his second in command and the coordinator of the operation targeting the Norte de Valle Cartel, Nathaniel Davidson and Martin Savoy, the US Military Attaché at the Embassy.

Chuck checked his watch. It was 1.58pm. Sean and Nat stared at the large screen at the end of the room. At 2pm exactly the phone in the middle of the table rang. Chuck answered it on the second ring and pressed the remote control. An image filled the screen of a room with eight people; seven men and one woman.

He instinctively straightened up as he saw the people who had been brought to the table in the DEA headquarters in Virginia. Included in the group were Phil Edwards, the Global Director of the DEA, John Nicholson, the Director of the DEA Special Operations Unit and Ronald Smith, the International Coordinator of the operations against the Norte de Valle Cartel as well as three US-based agents from the operation.

'It's good to see you all at today's meeting,' Chuck said.

'We're anxious to hear what you've been able to find out about the footage we sent you.'

'Thanks, Chuck. This is very important evidence your team has discovered and we have a solid analysis for you. But before we get started let me introduce you to two faces you may not know. Firstly, Claire Sparrows, newly appointed South America Operations Director with the CIA and Professor Carl Blunt, a world class specialist in Russian Submarines.' The DEA International Director, Phil Edwards, motioned to the woman to his right who smiled stiffly and then to the middle aged man to his left.

'Jumping straight to business,' the DEA Special Operations Unit Director, John Nicholson, said. 'We sent your video to several image and sound experts, and as you suspected the voices in the background are Russian. Our team was able to extract them from all ambient noises and we had several Russian language specialists analyse them. They all agreed that the accents were from north-east Russia.'

'So that's when we brought Professor Blunt in,' Phil Edwards said. 'We gave him the image of the submarine. With those images and the origin of the local engineers he has been able to identify what he believes to be the model of the submarine that has been assembled in Buenaventura. Carl, I'll hand it over to you to share your findings.'

'Thank you Phil. This is a great project to work on, fascinating but to be honest, it hasn't been easy. Just looking at the hull of the submarine from this angle you can't make out much,' The professor retrieved a pen from his shirt pocket and pointed to the blown up image of the submarine that he had in front of him. 'It looks to be around thirty to forty meters.'

'Do you know what type of submarine it is? Chuck asked.

'I know the model and possible builder of this very submarine,' he said. 'You see I had a vital piece of evidence to go on; it's likely that this came from north-east Russia. So, I sent some images to a contact of mine, who is ex-Russian navy and is now a professor of war studies in northern Russia. He knows every single submarine that was ever built. From analysing the image and some magnified images of the joining and body of the vessel he has come up with a match.'

The three men in the Bogota office were transfixed, their attention hanging on the professor's every word.

'So what type is it?' Nathaniel asked.

'It's an M-class, also known as Malyutka-class, which means "baby" in Russian,' the professor said. 'The Malyutka were a class of small submarines designed in the beginning of the 1930s as typical coastal submarines. They were intended to defend naval bases, blockade enemy harbours and, as a main feature, be railway friendly and easy to refit for transportation between different theatres of war. There were one hundred and forty of this class of submarine built.'

'Assuming your contact is right, tell us a bit about this submarine,' Chuck said. 'What's its internal capacity? How fast does it move? How deep does it dive?'

'These submarines are 37.5 meters long and has around a 270 cubic meter internal capacity. They run on diesel engines, travel at an average speed of 25 knots and can dive up to 200 metres.'

Chuck jotted down notes furiously while the professor rattled through his statistics and technical facts, and continued to make calculations after he finished. He stared at the numbers on his page, shaking his head.

'They could hold between five to ten thousand kilos of cocaine in that!'

'How on earth would they have gotten their hands on a submarine like this?' Sean Perry asked.

'I'm not sure,' Professor Blunt answered. 'But according to my contact, the Russian mafia has been known to have sold decommissioned submarines in the past. Apparently they have contacts or direct interests in formerly state-run shipping yards and scrap yards and probably work alongside corrupt sections of the military. But, my contact didn't have any concrete information. That's more your line of expertise.'

'Could a submarine that was built in the 1930s and presumably hasn't been used for years even run?' Chuck asked.

Professor Blunt shrugged. 'If the diesel engines are still in good shape, then technically yes.'

'You mentioned that the submarine was transported via rail in modules,' Nathaniel said. 'Do you think this came to Colombia in modules?'

'It definitely appears from the images that it is still being assembled.'

After Professor Blunt had answered all the questions and left the meeting, the DEA and CIA specialists were left to consider the ramifications of this new information.

'If the Professor's right, we're talking about a possible cargo capacity of 270 cubic metric tonnes that could fit at least 15,400 pounds of cocaine in one shipment, probably a lot more,' Chuck said. 'That would be one of the largest single shipments I've ever heard of.'

'Surely, the cartel's main contacts in the US will be involved in this operation,' Ronald Smith said, 'which means if we can follow it all the way to the US and track the drugs through delivery we could catch them red-handed.'

John Nicholson nodded. 'Yes. If we manage this we'll have enough evidence to arrest the cartel's main men in the US and Colombia, and hopefully get them to talk before El Magico disappears again.'

'Ideally we want to get a tracking device onboard somehow,' Chuck said.

'Do you have someone on the inside who could help us or is there anyone we could bring over to our side?' John asked.

Chuck glanced at Nat, who nodded slowly. 'We were put in touch with a young army electrician, specialising in electronics who was recently brought in to work on the fitout of the sub,' Nat said. 'Apparently he is terrified, but he's looking for a way to get out of the army while still helping his family. He has agreed to meet with us tomorrow.'

'An electronics engineer. Perfect!' Phil Edwards exclaimed.

'Offer him whatever he wants. If need be we can get him and his family into the US and set them up.'

He turned to address Claire Sparrows, the CIA agent. 'Would you be able to get us a tracking device with a signal strong enough to be traced underwater, that could last several months?'

Claire nodded. 'We should be able to do that, but we'd lose signal when it dives. However, that shouldn't be a problem as it will have to resurface at night and run the diesel engines to recharge its batteries.'

'Would it need to rely on the submarine's power?' Nathaniel asked.

'Ideally you'd wire it directly into the junction box in the control room so it can use the submarine's power,' Claire said.

'Does that mean we wouldn't have a signal until the submarine is launched?' Nathaniel asked. 'Obviously we'd prefer to be certain this is working before the sub is in the water.'

'We could provide the tracking device with a power pack to receive signal immediately.'

'That would be perfect,' Chuck said. 'How long would it last for?'

'It would send a signal every thirty minutes and could last up to two months,' she said. 'Do you want us to send someone down to Colombia to train your men to work the device?'

'That would help,' Chuck said. 'We have no idea when they're planning on moving this so we need to get a device onboard as soon as possible.'

'That shouldn't be a problem. We'll send an engineer down to help you and then set the monitoring up in the CIA offices in the embassy in Bogota.'

'It would be good to get regular satellite monitoring of the factory,' Chuck said. 'Phil, can you talk to South Com to see if they can help us?'

'Absolutely. The most important thing is to make sure we can monitor their progress and track the submarine without spooking them. How many people are aware of this operation?' Phil asked.

'Just the people in this room plus Jose Guevara who's running the Buenaventura operation with Nat,' Chuck said. 'A few others from our team in Bogota know that we're monitoring the situation in Buenaventura but they don't know the details. We haven't brought the Colombian Elite Police onboard yet.'

'Let's keep it that way. The fewer people involved, the less likely information leaks will occur,' Phil said. 'Your men in Buenaventura need to keep a very low profile.'

'I agree,' Chuck said. 'Minimal activity on the ground, especially in a place where it's so easy to stand out. Jose and Nat have started monitoring Pablo Ruiz and General Ordonez's phone communications and will reach out to the engineer. But we'll try to do the rest of the surveillance remotely.'

'Nathaniel, tell us about the people who provided this video. What do they want?' John Nicholson asked.

Nat glanced at Chuck. 'It's a bit of a strange case, sir. They don't want money or any of the regular demands. The girl's brother has been kidnapped by Pablo Ruiz's men and they came to us asking for our help.'

The men stared at him blankly.

'Well, did you put them in touch with the political section?' Ronald Smith asked.

'No. It's more complicated than that, sir. But of course we explained that there's very little we can do to help them.'

'Are they still in Buenaventura? I'm assuming the paramilitaries have no idea they took this video. They must be in danger.'

'The paramilitaries aren't aware that the video exists but are after them for information the girl's brother overheard and they relayed to the government. We've offered them support to get them to safety, but they refuse to leave until they get the brother back. They've asked us to get the rest of her family out of Buenaventura as they've been threatened so we've offered to organise a safe house in Bogota but they'll need to find a way to get there safely. Jose and I are in Cali tomorrow to meet the engineer.'

'Chuck, it sounds like your team has a lot on their hands,' John Nicholson said. 'Let us know what support you need. This is the best chance we've had in a long time to bring the Norte de Valle Cartel down. We can't afford to screw it up.'

Chuck nodded, all too aware of how important this operation was. This was the first time, to his knowledge, that the cartels had used proper submarines. The capacity to bring enormous amounts of cocaine into the US was immense. After a decade of chasing the Norte de Valle Cartel, this was one of the best opportunities he'd seen to really dismantle their networks in both the US and Colombia. A lot was riding on Nat's ability to convince the engineer to place the tracking device. It was a hell of a risk to ask him to take.

CHAPTER TWENTY-TWO

The two men sat in their black SUV in the B5 parking lot of the *Centenario* shopping center, one of the largest in Cali waiting for Mauricio.

'Do you think he's going to show?' Jose Guevara asked, pressing the light on his wristwatch to reveal the time. 'It's 9.30am. He's already an hour late.'

'He had better come,' Nathaniel said, cracking his knuckles as he surveyed the cars parked around them. 'The Director of the DEA is now following this operation and wants to know the results of this meeting.'

This was the biggest operation Nat had been put in charge of since joining the DEA. Hell, this was so big it might end up being discussed by the Congressional Foreign Affairs Committee his father chaired. The career politician might actually be interested in his dyslexic son's opinion for once. This was Nat's chance to prove himself to Chuck, who unlike his father, could see past his lack of academic success and that he was more than just a former Navy Seal. He could help devise and run a sophisticated operation to take down what might be the biggest, boldest plan any narco had come up with to traffic cocaine directly to the US.

The door opened. A couple appeared, arms entwined, laughing.

Jose whispered, 'Maybe he got freaked out. It's very dangerous, what we're asking him to do.'

'He doesn't know what we're asking him to do yet,' Nathaniel responded, his eyes fixed on the door.

'Sure, but just meeting with us would be risky, which is clearly why he wanted to meet here in Cali, in this place.'

The door opened again, and a tall slim man appeared. He stopped and looked around the parking lot, his eyes darting from car to car. He stepped forward as if walking on newly frozen ice. His head jerked between the cars and the door.

'That's got to be him,' Nathaniel said, opening the door and standing to wave at the man. 'Mauricio?'

The man looked around him again before nodding.

'I'm Nathaniel and this is Jose who you talked to on the phone. Do you want to get into the car? It will be safer and more private.'

He dashed over. 'Let's get out of here.'

'Where to?' Nathaniel asked, turning around to face the man who had slumped on the back seat. He had a boyish face, probably no older than his mid-twenties. He fidgeted; his eyes continued darting from one side to the other.

'Anywhere. Just drive. I want to be sure I haven't been followed.'

Nathaniel pulled out and the headlights washed over a young man stepping into the parking lot. Mauricio doubled over.

'Do you know him?' Nathaniel asked, pushing down the central lock and watching the man in the rear-view mirror.

'No. But he might have been sent to follow me,' Mauricio whispered. 'Is he still behind us?'

'He's gone,' Nathaniel said. 'Why do you think someone is following you?'

'Ever since I started working in the factory I feel like I'm being watched. They barely let any of us out of their sight. They're paranoid.'

'So how'd you manage to get to Cali?'

'When the General offered me the job and said I'd have to work every weekend I told him that I needed this weekend off as it is my mother's birthday and I always come to see her. It was my only condition.'

'So your mother lives around here?' Nathaniel asked.

'Yeah, in Agua Blanca. Do you know it?'

Nathaniel nodded. It was the poorest area in Cali, where the majority of the residents were displaced by the war. The crime rate was high and government presence scarce. 'So you take care of your mother?'

'And my three younger sisters.'

They left the car park and headed through the center of the city. Dozens of yellow taxis and motorbikes hustled the streets. Multi-colored neon lights and loud salsa music enticed people into the different clubs that lined the sidewalk.

'That must be tough,' Jose said.

'It's my family. I'd do anything for them.'

Nat glanced at the man in the rear-view mirror. He hadn't seen his own brother in nearly five years. Of course, he'd heard about him on the rare occasions he spoke to his parents. They were always eager to boast of the family's Harvard graduate's up and coming political career.

After driving for fifteen minutes Nathaniel turned the car off the main road and wound its way through the quiet historic neighborhood of San Antonio. He pulled up on a street that was empty apart from two parked cars.

'Is this okay?' he asked, looking at Mauricio in the rear-view mirror.

Mauricio glanced around the area before nodding. Nathaniel killed the engine and turned to face him.

'We hear you're looking for a way to get out of the army and to help your family,' he said, trying to make eye contact, but it was difficult to catch Mauricio's shifting gaze.

'Other soldiers who have tried to speak up about what they've seen have had accidents,' Mauricio said with an emphasis on the last word. 'I want out, but it's too hard, especially now.'

'What do you mean by that?' Jose asked.

'Ever since I've been working at the factory,' Mauricio stopped as a motorbike turned onto the street, continuing only when it was out of sight. 'They pay us much better than my normal job with the army, but like I said before, they're paranoid. They want us to work around the clock and they're constantly drilling into us that we can't talk to anyone about what's going on or they'll kill us and our family.'

Jose glanced at Nathaniel, wincing slightly.

'So you feel trapped. You want to get out and continue to help your family, but don't know how to do that,' Nathaniel said.

'Exactly. Diana seemed to think you could help me. But really I could be killed for talking to you.'

Nathaniel studied Mauricio. He had to offer him something good in order to break through the fear that so obviously gripped him. 'Would you like to be able to get you and your family out of Colombia and go somewhere safe?'

Mauricio looked straight at him for the first time, his eyes narrowing. 'What do you mean?'

'We need your help and we're willing to pay you very well for it.'

'You want to know what they're building in the factory?'

'No, we already know they're building a submarine so they can export millions of dollars' worth of cocaine to the US.'

'That's what it's for. I figured as much. And the General is involved in that as well?' Mauricio said, shaking his head.

'It certainly seems that way. Wasn't it the General who put you in this position?'

Mauricio nodded. 'If you know what's going on why do you need me?'

Nathaniel hesitated, wondering how to best frame the answer. But the truth was what they were asking for was inherently dangerous and there was no real way to make it seem otherwise.

'We need someone on the inside to put a tracking device on the submarine.'

'A tracking device?' Mauricio's voice rose several octaves. 'That would be absolute suicide. You might as well kill me now.'

'It doesn't have to be that hard, Mauricio,' Jose said. 'What stage are you at with the submarine wiring?'

'We're at the final stages of connecting the wiring harnesses from one module to the other. As soon as that's complete we'll do a final check of the junction boxes and connect the batteries. From there we just need to do continuity checks to make sure it's all working and fix any glitches.'

'When will you be working on the junction boxes?' Nathaniel asked.

'If everything goes smoothly, it should be in a few days,' Mauricio said. 'Look, what you're asking is too dangerous and I could get killed just for talking to you. I think I've told you enough.'

'Mauricio, hear us out,' Nathaniel said. 'The tracking device is very small. It's around two by two inches, which is the size of a matchbox. You could wire it to the junction box around the region of the conning tower. You'll be working on it anyway so no-one should notice.'

'But if they found out I'd be killed on the spot.'

'They won't find out. Like I said, it's so small and will be easily disguised amongst the wiring in the junction box,' Nathaniel said. 'You can attach it while doing your normal work so it wouldn't be anything out of the ordinary.'

Mauricio shook his head vigorously. 'It's too dangerous. I can't do it.'

'But, Mauricio, you work on the submarine nearly every day. It would be so easy for you. No-one would ever notice,' Nathaniel said. 'In return we're offering you the opportunity to take your family and set up a new life in the US.'

'In the US?' Mauricio asked slowly.

'If you do this for us and successfully attach the device we'll relocate you and your family to the US with special visas to establish a new life there and enough money to live comfortably.'

Mauricio's mouth was agape. 'Are you serious?'

'Absolutely.' Nathaniel knew they had him.

'But what about my girlfriend and her daughter? I couldn't leave without them.'

'This request comes from high up. If you put the device on the submarine and keep us updated about the progress in the factory we will include your girlfriend and her daughter,' Nathaniel said.

'But how long would I have to stay working in the factory?'

'Until it's launched or close to the time. We can't risk them getting suspicious if you leave beforehand. When do you think that will be?'

'I think they want to launch in a matter of weeks. But if I were to do this I wouldn't want to stay around and risk them finding the device. I'd want to get out straightaway.'

'They're not going to find it,' Nathaniel said. 'We will train you on how to install it. The device will be virtually undetectable. If anything were to happen we would get you out earlier.'

'We're talking about giving you a whole new life,' Jose said.

'You wouldn't have to worry anymore.'

'How do I know you're telling the truth?'

'We can put it in writing with an official stamp from the US government and we can start the process of the visas, at least for your family.'

Mauricio stared out the window at the enormous houses further up the hill. 'How much money will you give us?'

Nathaniel decided to jump straight to the high end of what he'd discussed with Chuck. He needed this man. 'A million dollars.'

'A million dollars!' Mauricio looked like a dumbstruck child.

Nathaniel nodded.

'What happens if I'm killed? Will you still give this to my family?'

Nathaniel thought of his family and felt a pang of guilt. He only contacted them when he had an achievement to report, which compared to his brother wasn't that often. He certainly didn't go home for his mother's birthday and he couldn't imagine making the decision to put his life in serious danger in order to guarantee them financial security. But this was the decision Mauricio was making. Nathaniel hoped it didn't come to that.

'If you help us, we will take care of you and your family, no matter what.'

'Fine, I'll do it,' Mauricio said, a slight tremor in his voice.

Nathaniel breathed a sigh of relief. He and Jose had just secured the DEA's way into the factory and the submarine. His bosses in Bogota and Virginia would be pleased. But his excitement was dulled by his genuine fear for Mauricio's life. The man was right. What they were asking him to do was extremely dangerous. He would be killed if caught. Something about the man's willingness to sacrifice himself for his family humbled Nathaniel. Mauricio was putting his life in their hands. He hoped they didn't let him down. But he knew he couldn't promise anything.

CHAPTER TWENTY-THREE

'Do you think Jhon Jairo will help us?' Luzma asked Rafa. Her family only had two days left before the paramilitaries made good their threat, and they were running out of options. Nathaniel and Jose from the DEA were out of town and although they said they could help, they wouldn't be back before Friday. So they were going to set Luzma's family up in a safe house in Bogota. But first, she needed to find a way to get them out of Buenaventura safely.

'I don't know.' Rafa concentrated on the road in front of him, weaving the car around the frantic early morning traffic. 'It's a lot to ask and very dangerous.'

'He's our only hope. If we don't get my family out by Friday they'll be killed.' The words were almost too painful to articulate.

Horns honked impatiently. Another vehicle swerved in front of the car. Rafa braked suddenly and they were both jolted forward.

'I know, Luzma,' he replied, tersely.

Rafa pulled the car over in front of the entrance to the *Universidad de Valle*. Jhon Jairo was waiting, his bright orange jacket hugging his broad shoulders and his worker's helmet tucked under his arm. It was the same uniform he had worn all the times Luzma had met him before in the human rights meetings she had attended with Rafa. He eased himself into the back seat slowly. His back was hunched. The twenty-five years of heavy labor on the docks had affected his spine.

'I heard what happened to your brother,' he said awkwardly, his calloused hand gently touching Luzma's arm for a moment. 'I'm sorry. I hope you can get him back.'

'We're trying, but now I have another problem and we were hoping you could help us,' she said, very aware that she probably only had five or ten minutes to guarantee his help.

Jhon Jairo looked at her, concerned. 'Sure if you think I can help,' he said with a shrug.

'The paramilitaries have threatened the rest of my family. They've said that if I don't present myself to them by Friday they'll kill them.'

'Obviously if Luzma goes to the paras they will kill her so that's not an option,' Rafa said, glancing at her.

'We need to get them out of Buenaventura,' Luzma said.

'Travelling by canoe or speed boat along the rivers is dangerous because the paras, the guerrilla and the army are fighting over so much of that territory. Travelling by bus or car could also be dangerous because of all the checkpoints. We know that General Ordonez is involved and has Jolene's house monitored and phones tapped. So it's quite possible that my family's names and photos could be on a 'no pass' list.'

Luzma studied Jhon Jairo's face, silently urging him to help. He looked at her, shifting in his seat slightly.

'We were wondering if you have any truck driver friends who will be leaving Buenaventura before Friday,' she asked

'Yeah, I know quite a few of them. But what do you have in mind?'

'We thought maybe Grandma, Grandpa and Aunt Jolene could hide in one of those and get off in Bogota where we have people who will help them.'

Jairo looked out the window. In front of them, army officers stood at either side of the bridge that led from the mainland to the island where the port was located. Their bodies appeared hulk-like under the full army fatigues. Luzma turned so that her back faced the window. Rafa pulled the black cap he wore further down over his forehead and stared ahead. The monstrous cranes and the mountains of multicolored containers in the port loomed to the side.

'It's a lot to ask them,' Jairo said. 'If they were caught they could lose their licence and that's their only source of income. If the paramilitaries find out that they have helped they could be targeted too.'

Luzma desperately scrambled to think of ways she could convince him. 'But we could hide them so it would be very hard to find them.' Her voice cracked with emotion. 'Jairo, if I don't get them out of here before Friday they will be killed and I would prefer to hand myself in to the paramilitaries rather than let that happen.'

Luzma glanced at Rafa, imploring him to say something. She knew he was uncomfortable putting Jairo in this situation. Rafa had helped him put pressure on the government to improve the situation at the port and get international support when individual workers were unduly sacked or threatened. Luzma was desperately hoping he would call in a favour. 'Brother, I'm sorry. I really don't want to create any problems for you...'

Jairo nodded slowly. 'Okay, I have one friend who I think might be able to help. I can call him now to see when his next shift is.'

'Thank you so much,' Luzma said.

'Don't thank me yet. We don't know if he'll do it.'

Jairo dialled a number and started talking.

Please God; help me save my family, Luzma pleaded silently. *I'll do anything you want if you just help me keep Jair, Grandma, Grandpa and Aunt Jolene safe.*

Jairo seemed to be trying to convince his friend. Luzma clenched her hands and tried to distract herself by looking at the busy road, the tightly huddled shops and the bustling sidewalk. But it was impossible to really think of anything else. Time stretched out painfully, every passing minute dragged.

After what felt like an eternity there was silence. She stared at Jairo.

'He's a very good man, a friend from the union. Someone who will always help people,' he said. 'He has agreed to take your family.'

'Thank God! Thank you so much. When can they leave?' The words seemed to fly out of her mouth, the relief making her babble.

'His next shift is Thursday leaving in the night.'

'Thursday? Is that the earliest? Can you make it any earlier? The paramilitaries said I had until Friday. That means leaving it until the last minute.'

'That's the best I can do,' Jairo said.

'I'm sorry.' She felt bad for pushing the man further. She was asking someone else to put their life at risk to help her family. 'I really appreciate your help. What time does he leave and how can we get them on the truck?'

'He said he'll be leaving late afternoon or early evening. He could stop briefly at some shops on the outskirts of the city. There are fewer people there so they could get in quickly undetected. I have to call him back tomorrow to organize the details. I have to go to work and you shouldn't drive any further if you're trying to avoid the military. This area is crawling with them.'

'Have you spoken to my family?' Luzma asked as soon as Daniela and Mario from the local Afro-Colombian organisation walked in.

Luzma and Rafa were meeting with Daniela and Mario in an empty room at the school where Daniela taught. They were close friends with Rafa and Aunty Jolene and they both lived in San Francisco so they were able to get news to and from her family. The sounds outside contrasted to those pounding in Luzma's head. Children's excited voices, laughter and gleeful screams mingled together.

'Yes, we've talked to them,' Mario said. 'They said they'd leave if you do, but they want to know how we're going to get Jair back first. They're so worried about you both.'

'First, let's figure out how to get them out because we only have today and tomorrow and then we'll figure out a plan to rescue Jair,' Luzma said. She already had an idea of how to get Jair back, but it was a plan that was too dangerous to voice until her family was safely out of Buenaventura.

'We need to get them out by tomorrow night,' Daniela said, sitting down at one of the classroom tables. 'What do you have in mind?'

'Jhon Jairo has arranged for one of his friends, a truck driver, to pick them up on the outskirts of town at the shops about three kilometres before you reach the first checkpoint,' Luzma said. 'He's going to hide them among the goods he's transporting to Bogota. He'll drop them off there and then the men we met from the US government have agreed to organize a safe place for them to stay.'

'That's a big favour,' Mario said. 'How do we get them from San Francisco, where the house is guarded and the whole place is crawling with paras, to this meeting point?'

If the paramilitaries found out her family were trying to escape they would be slaughtered on the spot.

'We don't know. We're hoping you can help us figure that out,' Luzma said.

'Just how tightly are the paras watching them at the moment?' Rafa asked.

Daniela's mouth tightened and she glanced at Mario.

'They've set up a little "Dominoes Club" on the corner similar to what you see in Los Lleres, so a group of kids watch whoever comes in and out of the street. If anyone leaves they ask where they're going and follow them. They don't let them go anywhere alone,' Mario said.

Luzma's stomach lurched. How could they possibly get them out in that situation? She stood up and started pacing around the classroom. She needed to calm her mind in order to think clearly. 'What about when Grandpa goes out on the fishing boat?'

Mario shook his head. 'They're not allowing him to go.'

She couldn't imagine Grandpa not fishing. He had never missed a day in his life. It was his profession, but also his love. How were they eating without any income to buy food?

'Are they allowed to leave the house?'

'Sometimes, but as I said, they're interrogated as to where they're going and then they are followed,' Daniela said.

Luzma's family were prisoners and she couldn't think of how they could possibly escape unnoticed. If they didn't get out by tomorrow they would be killed anyway. She looked at Rafa for inspiration, but he stared out the window.

'How are we going to get them out?' Luzma said, half to herself. She stood at the window looking at the neighborhoods below. 'Where is the tide in the late afternoon?'

'It's just starting to come in. Why?' Mario asked.

'It's disgusting, but they could walk underneath the houses if the tide hasn't come in. They could get down there from the back balcony without being noticed and then walk under the houses. We'd need to get them to a home on a street that's not being guarded and organize a car to pick them up from there.' She sat back at the table, looking expectantly at the others.

'It could work, but we need someone in the community who has a car,' Mario said. 'They're very suspicious of any new people or vehicles in the area and taxis rarely go into the community anymore.'

'What about old Jorge Caldas?' Daniela asked. 'They've allowed him to keep operating his taxi and he's very close to Jolene after all the help she's given him.'

'Ah yes,' Mario said. 'And maybe we could ask Daisy from the women's group to help. She lives on a side street about six blocks from Jolene's house. We could get her and her family to take the taxi and your grandparents and Jolene to hide in the boot or the backseat.'

Excitement began to replace the anguish. They could do this. 'Do you think it would work?' Luzma asked.

Mario shrugged and motioned with open hands. 'I think anything we try is going to be risky because the paras control the area completely. But if they've said they will start killing them on Friday,' he paused and shrugged slightly, 'well, I think it's our best option and we have to go for it.'

It wasn't exactly the reassuring vote of confidence Luzma was hoping for, but it was the truth.

'How do we organize this?' Rafa asked.

'We can talk to Jorge Caldas and Daisy this afternoon,' Mario said. 'Once we've confirmed with them, we'll get a message to Luzma's family with the plan. Call us tonight on the new number I gave you so we can confirm. Meanwhile you organize everything with Jhon Jairo and the driver.'

'Thank you so much.' Luzma reached across the table to take Daniela and Mario's hands. 'I can't tell you how grateful I am.'

'Next we have to figure out how to get Jair and that's going to be much more difficult,' Daniela said.

CHAPTER TWENTY-FOUR

Mauricio reached into his pocket, his long fingers ferreting out the device that could get him killed. His calloused fingertips found the cold, smooth surface. It was no bigger than a box of matches, but it felt like lead in the pocket of his track pants.

He only had thirty minutes, if he was lucky. The head Russian engineer and his colleague had gone to lunch, leaving Mauricio to finish running cables from module three to the control room. It was the only chance he would get without them around.

He dipped his head to step through the hatch into the control room. The periscope took up the middle of the small cramped space and the rest was jammed full of high pressure piping, ageing brass instruments and looms of wiring. Mauricio had always found the space claustrophobic. Today it felt even more so.

The junction box he was after, that joined the wiring from the control room to the conning tower, was above him. Sweat dripped down his back. Was he crazy? If he was caught he would be killed. Then again, how else would he be able to help his family escape the constant danger and poverty that they lived in? This was the best chance he had to provide for them like his father would have wanted.

The door of the junction box was opened, revealing masses of cables from the control room that were joined by connecters to reciprocal cables leading to the conning tower. The wiring looms were directed through glands in the bulkhead which would later be sealed.

The US agents had told him that the tracking device needed to connect to the submarine's power sources within the junction box closest to the conning tower. The device had its own battery, but that would only last a month or two and would then need to use the submarine's power. They had advised him to hide the device amongst the wiring and run the antenna through a gland up into the conning tower in order for it to have best reception.

Looking at the looms of wire before him, he wondered where on earth he could safely hide the device.

Mauricio checked his watch. If he was going to do this he needed to act now. He stepped back to glance through the forward and aft hatches. It was all clear.

He took a deep breath and tried to think of his family; of his dear stoic mother, whose eyes seemed to sink farther into her head every year. She never spoke about the pain of losing her husband or struggling to care for her family despite living in an area ablaze with an underground war. He would do nearly anything to get her and his three sisters out of the squalor and violence they lived in.

He searched among the looms of cables arriving and leaving the junction box and found a place to hide the tracker. From there he could connect it to the submarine's 24-volt power supply. He then followed the cables going through the glands to the conning tower to find where to hide the antenna. Several cables in the loom were black as was the antenna, so, hopefully it would be concealed.

He took one more look around. There was no sign of the Russians. He strained to listen over the top of the buzz and banging of the welding and hammering that was going on in the other modules. His hands shook as he pulled the device from his pocket. He had to stay focused on why he was doing this.

He pulled back looms of wires and placed the tracker behind them. He wired the positive and negative lines into their respective terminals.

With the device attached to the power source, he pulled out the antenna, which was about two metres long. He found the end point and began to thread it into the loom leading to the conning tower.

Suddenly he heard the head Russian engineer's distinctive laugh above the production noise. His body felt cold. A metre of the antenna cable still hung out of the junction box.

He stepped back to look through the hatch. The Russian's back was towards him, talking to someone in the second module. His heart raced wildly. He tried to ram the rest of the antenna through the loom, but his hands were shaking so badly he could barely do it.

'Mauricio,' the Russian called out from the adjoining module.

Mauricio pushed the remainder of the antenna into the loom and pulled back the wires as he had found them.

'I didn't tell you to work on that,' The Russian said in his thick accent. 'What are you doing?'

Mauricio stuffed his hands into his pockets to hide the shaking and turned slowly.

The Russian stared at him, waiting for an answer.

'Sorry, sir.' Mauricio hoped his voice would not reveal the fear he felt. 'I was getting confused by the wiring diagram and was trying to figure out the direction of these cables from the third module to the conning tower.'

The Russian stepped over to Mauricio. He stared at the junction box. Would he be able to see a difference?

The Russian reached up to the wiring near where the device was hidden. The thumping of Mauricio's heart was deafening.

And then the Russian smiled and slapped Mauricio on the back.

'Don't look so scared,' he said. 'I don't expect you to know everything about how this baby works. That's why I'm here.'

CHAPTER TWENTY-FIVE

'They'll be here. Don't worry,' Rafa said.

'It's 6.30. We said 6.00,' Luzma replied, pacing back and forth in the car park behind the small store. The sun was quickly sinking behind the mountains to the west, casting long shadows behind the small buildings.

Three trucks rolled past. Luzma willed them to pull into the meeting area, but they continued. What if Jhon Jairo's friend was spooked and decided not to help them? She strained to hear if any more vehicles were coming but the only noise was the river below rushing past and the twittering of birds in the surrounding jungle.

Luzma's ears pricked at the sound of an engine approaching. An enormous truck came around the corner.

'Please be him,' she whispered.

The truck slowed and then pulled into the meeting spot. Her muscles unclenched slightly.

'Luz Marina?' the middle-aged man asked as he stepped down from the truck and looked around.

'Don Hernao, thank you so much for helping my family. You don't know how grateful I am.'

'I do what I can to help,' he said simply. 'Where are they?'

She shuffled uncomfortably, wishing she knew.

'They're not here yet but they're definitely coming'

'I can't stay here long. People will start to talk, the army might pass, I have a schedule I have to keep and I'm already late.' The light from inside the truck highlighted Mr Henao's face and as he spoke, lines of worry were etched on his forehead. He looked at his watch and shook his head.

'I have to leave by 7.30 at the latest. If they're not here by then, I'll have to go without them.'

The tightness in Luzma's chest returned. 'They'll be here by then.'

Mr Henao walked to the small store where a woman was selling fried chorizo, plantains and packet food. Luzma returned to the car to talk to Rafa.

'We have to call Mario and Daniela to find out what's happening. If they don't get here soon he'll leave without them.'

'They're going to be here, don't worry,' Rafa said, putting his arm around her. 'We agreed that if there was any problem they would call us on the phone Sister Clara lent us. They haven't called, so that's a good sign.'

She pulled away, unable to stand still. 'Didn't you hear what I said? He's going to leave without them at 7.30.'

'Luzma, you know that their phones are probably tapped. If we call them we could all get caught.'

Just then the sound of an engine approached. Lights came around the corner and highlighted the side of the truck. Suddenly Rafa yanked Luzma down behind the car.

'It's the police,' he whispered.

Her heart lurched. What were they doing here? Had they found Grandma and Grandpa and were now coming for Rafa and her? The car pulled up beside the truck and footsteps crunched across the gravel. Luzma peeked under the car. Men's boots walked towards the shop. She laid down pressing her face against the dirt to see under the car. Everything was black apart from the light from the store. She could make out Mr Henao leaning against the side of the shop, a bottle in his hand. The police presence would surely spook him.

'Good evening, Officers,' Mr Henao said as the two men stepped before him.

'Are you on your way in or out?' one of the officers asked.

'Out,' Mr Henao responded. 'But I'm feeling a bit rough after last night so I need a *Pony Malta* and some food before I hit the road.'

More silence. Some of the dust began to scratch Luzma's throat. She desperately wanted to cough but didn't dare.

'Could we see your papers?' one of the officers asked.

God, Orishas please help. Mr Henao is my only chance of getting my family out of Buenaventura. Please allow them to travel to safety.

The sound of another engine grew louder and lights washed across the parking lot as the vehicle rounded the corner. Were they sending more men? The vehicle slowed down. Could it be her family? If they stopped now they would be caught by the police. She strained to make out the vehicle but her view was blocked by the truck. The car engine grew distant. The truck door clicked open and there was a rustle of papers.

'Here you go, sir,' Mr Henao said.

More silence, grating against Luzma's unravelled nerves like the dust in her throat.

'Okay, Mr Henao. Your papers are in order. You should be getting on though. You've got a long trip ahead.'

'Yes, sir. I will get my food and hit the road.'

The boots turned and walked towards the police car. The engine came to life and the tyres spun as the car pulled out onto the road. Luzma exhaled.

'Man, that had me worried,' Rafa whispered.

'There's no way he's going to stay around now.' Luzma scrambled to her feet, wiping the dust off the side of her face and coughing it from her lungs. 'We have to call them, Rafa. I'm sure Mr Henao is going to want to leave straightaway. He won't want to risk the officers coming back.'

An engine rumbled towards them from the direction the army officers had just headed. Mr Henao stood at the front of the store, supplies in hand and looked towards the direction of the engine. He started to head towards the truck. If he left, Luzma had little chance of getting her family out of Buenaventura that night. She had to stop him, but didn't want to be caught in the open if it were the police returning. He opened the truck door.

'Mr Henao, wait please,' she cried.

Car lights swept across the lot and Rafa tried to yank her down behind the car. She pushed him off and headed for Mr Henao. A taxi pulled up beside the truck.

'Thank God.' Luzma ran to the car.

An old man stepped out of the driver's seat. She stepped passed him and looked into the car. A family that she didn't recognize was packed into the taxi but no sign of her family.

'You must be Luzma,' the old man said, walking around to the trunk. As he opened it the faint light from the car and the cabin of the truck revealed two bodies curled around each other.

'Grandma, Grandpa.' A surge of love and relief filled her.

She helped them slowly prise themselves from the trunk, marvelling that they had been able to fit in there. They hugged each other so tightly that she could barely breathe. Tears slid down her face, despite her efforts to hold them back.

'Thank God, you're all right,' she whispered.

Grandma whispered a prayer as she rocked Luzma.

'Where's Aunt Jolene?' Luzma asked, looking around.

Grandma wiped away tears with the back of her hand. 'She refused to come. She said she needed to stay with the community to help them, but insisted that we go.'

'No, she has to leave now. We have to find Jolene and get her out of here.'

Mr Henao came around the corner. 'I'm sorry I can't stay any longer. We have to get them in the truck and get out of here now.'

'Yes, I'm sorry. Thank you so much for waiting' Luzma whispered.

He opened the doors to the back of the truck.

'Don't worry, I'll get Aunt Jolene out of here as well and I promise I'll find Jair.'

'What are you talking about?' Grandpa asked. 'You're coming with us. We're not leaving without you.'

Luzma took in a deep breath. She had to be strong for them. She had never lied to her grandparents, but it was the only way they would leave.

'I have a plan to get Jair back and I have help from the US government so. We're not in danger. But I can't do it if the paramilitaries are threatening to kill you. If you stay, I will have to give myself in and they'll probably kill me and Jair. By leaving, you are saving our lives.'

Grandpa shook his head. 'You are just like your mother.'

His words filled her heart. It was the best compliment she had ever received and it meant so much that it had come from him, a man who said few words.

'We will stay and help you,' Grandma said. 'We're not leaving you alone.'

'No, I'll stay and find Jair and you leave with your grandmother,' Grandpa said. 'I'm not going to lose another loved one.'

'As I said, I have it all organized with the Americans. But they won't let us all stay with them and I know them. This is our best chance to save Jair. You need to leave now and we'll see each other in Bogota within a week, I promise.'

'We can't leave without you,' Grandma repeated.

Mr Henao cleared his throat as he looked at his watch.

'Grandma, if you want to help Jair you need to leave, there is no other way.'

Grandma shook her head. 'Promise me that the US government is protecting you and you'll be safe.'

'Promise,' Luzma said leading them to the truck with Grandma sobbing as she hugged Luzma again.

'May God protect you both,' Grandma said as she heaved herself into the back of the truck with Grandpa's help.

CHAPTER TWENTY-SIX

Pablo lay back on the single sofa watching hardcore pornography while Carlos and two others huddled together on the couch.

One of his men, who had just clocked off from his shift, came in. He smiled as he took in the images on the screen. He headed for the fridge that stood in the middle of the lounge room.

'Throw me a beer,' Pablo said.

Pablo took a sip, taking in some more of the images on the screen and then turned to the young man. 'So, how's it going? Have you seen anything out of the ordinary?'

Pablo had organized surveillance on all the outsiders who were working on the submarine. He had too much riding on this project. He couldn't take any risks and he certainly didn't trust anyone who was not in his inner circle to keep the submarine a secret.

'Carlos tells me you got a trip to Cali,' he said. 'I hope you were working and not partying it up with the Cali girls.'

'No, boss, no partying,' the man said. 'Just following the electrician. He's such a mummy's boy. He does have some hot sisters though. I wouldn't mind doing one of them!'

Pablo laughed and returned to watching the porn. The house, seized from the former owner of the factory, had proven a very useful den to entertain his men and keep them away from town where they might be tempted to speak about the submarine. Here he provided everything they needed: women, booze, drugs, food and beds. The smell of stale smoke, alcohol and sweat permeated the air, but they didn't mind as long as their basic needs were met.

'The electrician has a very hot girlfriend in Buenaventura,' the young man said. 'Mind you, that didn't stop him getting some while he was Cali.'

Pablo's attention was focused on the threesome on the screen.

'Did he pick up a street girl while he was there?'

'I'm not sure. I followed him to one of the big malls in Cali. He headed straight for the parking lot, but then he disappeared. I imagine he was getting it on with one of the chicks there, or maybe he's a *maricka*.'

Pablo turned to face the man. 'So you lost him?'

'Well, yes, but only for a few hours. I went back to his house and he turned up there three hours later.'

'You have no idea what he did for three hours,' Pablo said. He could feel the heat rising in his face as he stared at the incompetent man before him.

The man looked around him and then back at Pablo. 'Yes, sir. But I was following him. It's just he disappeared very quickly once he got to the car park. But I'm sure he was just going to get a blow job.'

'A three-hour blow job?'

The man shrugged.

'Do you not take your job seriously?' Pablo's tone became menacing. He enjoyed watching the man squirm in front of him.

'Yes, sir. I know it's very important. I won't let him out of my sight again, sir.'

'When you're working I want you to know everything he does and says and every single person he speaks to. If I hear that you've lost him again, you're in trouble. Are you clear?'

'Yes, sir.'

CHAPTER TWENTY-SEVEN

Something was wrong. Luzma could feel it. She had learned over the years that her intuition was nearly always right. She scanned the street below for something unusual. Aunty Jolene shuffled across the road towards the church where she was scheduled to speak at a community meeting. She wore her trademark African-print scarf around her head and a bright red long dress that ruffled in the wind.

Luzma watched from the second-storey window. Mario had sneaked her into a room in his friend's cheap motel in the centre of town. Daniela would give the word to Aunty Jolene to meet her there. That was the plan, at least.

Who were the men standing huddled in front of the church? Who was the teenage boy slinking behind Jolene? Then Luzma saw the motorbike swerving in and out of the traffic towards her aunt. The man wore a helmet, something uncommon in Buenaventura, and he wasn't wearing the mandatory jacket that showed the bike's number plates.

'Jolene, run!' Luzma shouted, but her words were washed out by the thumping music and horns below.

The motorbike was less than ten metres away from Jolene and was heading straight towards her.

'What's wrong?' Mario asked.

Luzma calculated the distance between the second floor room where she stood and Jolene. There was no way she could make it before the motorbike reached her.

'Call Jolene and tell her to move now,' she shouted.

Mario looked at her and then dialed the number. The motorbike moved between the cars, getting dangerously close. Jolene reached into her bag, y trying to find her phone.

'Pick it up!' Luzma shouted and then looked towards the heavens.

'God, please do something. Please help her.'

Jolene had her phone and was putting it to her ear. The motorbike was just behind her. The man reached into his jacket. Luzma grabbed the phone from Mario.

'Aunty, move now!' she shouted.

'Hello. Who is it?' Jolene asked, yelling over the top of the noise.

The man on the motorbike lifted a gun out of his jacket and pointed it towards Jolene's head.

'Jolene duck!' Luzma shouted desperately into the phone.

Suddenly Jolene lurched forward, falling into the crowd.

'No,' Luzma shrieked. Her legs buckled and she grabbed for the wall to support herself.

The man fired one more shot, hitting Jolene in the chest. He then swerved onto the sidewalk and sped away.

Luzma sprinted for the door, taking the steps down the fire exit two at a time.

'Luzma stop!' Mario shouted.

Luzma didn't listen. She had to get to her aunt. She burst through the door that led to the lobby of the hotel and onto the road. Outside people were running for cover in the hotel and shops. Luzma pushed against them.

Through the frantic crowd Luzma could see her aunt crumpled on the road. A pool of blood as red as her dress slowly ran out across the pavement.

She was just two meters from her aunt when a hand gripped her shoulder. She turned around to see Mario behind her, his face pale.

'There's nothing we can do for her now. It's too late.'

Luzma pushed his hand away and bent down next to her aunt. She felt for Jolene's pulse. There was none.

'Luzma, we have to get you out of here or you'll be next,' Mario said, pulling her up.

Sirens wailed in the background. Luzma looked down at her hands. They were stained with her aunty's blood.

'Luzma, we have to leave now. This place is crawling with paramilitaries and the military will be here any minute now.'

The air was so heavy with misery that Luzma found it hard to breathe. The small room in the nun's retreat centre on the outskirts of town, pressed in on her like a prison cell with its grey cement walls. The only light came from a tiny window near the ceiling, revealing the rain that had started.

Luzma, Rafa, Mario, Daniela and Sister Clara sat in silence. Occasionally Daniela or Sister Clara would begin crying again. But Luzma had no more tears left. Her sorrow was mixed with rage. How could they kill such a beautiful person? Her aunt had dedicated her life to helping others and sacrificed so much to do so.

The image of what had happened a few hours ago haunted her. How easy it had been for the man who killed her. Did he even think about what he was doing? The cement beneath Luzma's feet felt like ice and a shiver ran through her. The paramilitaries and their friends were inhumane and would do whatever it took to silence anyone who got in their way. How many more days could she and Rafa stay alive when the paras controlled half of the city and were clearly determined to kill them? How much longer would they keep Jair alive? Maybe he wasn't even alive.

The only thing that brought Luzma any solace was knowing that her grandparents were safe. Rafa had checked with the men from the US government and they had picked them up in Bogota. If only Jolene had left with them. She should have gone to Jolene last night to convince her to leave. Maybe then her aunt would still be alive.

Mario broke the long silence. 'You two really need to leave Buenaventura. It's not safe.'

'Yes, the paramilitaries have made it perfectly clear that they want you dead, Luzma,' Sister Clara said. 'If you don't leave they will find you sooner or later.'

'It's not just Luzma,' Mario said. 'Rafa is also in serious danger because they know he's helping her. I would normally think you were safe as a foreigner, but not anymore.'

Luzma looked at the faces of the people around her. She had only known Rafa, Sister Clara, Daniela and Mario for several months but they were risking their lives to help her. She couldn't let them do that anymore. She needed to do the rest alone.

'Luzma,' Rafa said, reaching to take her hand. 'They're right. It's too dangerous for us to stay here.'

She nodded.

'You're right. I'm sorry I've gotten you into this,' she said.

'It's too dangerous now. You need to leave.'

She wished she could also leave, to escape this nightmare. The thought of facing these men alone terrified her. But she would not leave Jair and she couldn't let them continue to get away with this violence.

Rafa stared at her. '*We* need to leave. Not just me.'

'I can't leave without Jair,' she said, shaking her head.

'Luzma, we can help Jair from Bogota,' Rafa replied. 'We don't need to be here. The only thing we're doing by staying is making it easier for them to kill us.'

Luzma ignored him. She couldn't entertain the idea of escaping to safety. She had to get Jair back and she knew the only way she was going to do it was by being in Buenaventura.

'You need to call Nathaniel and Jose. They said they could help us get out of Buenaventura. Tell them you need to get out tonight.'

'Luzma, you're not listening to me. You can't stay either.'

'Rafa, I don't have a choice. I'm staying. End of story.'

'Luzma, stop being so goddamn stubborn. You will be killed if you stay. Is that what you want?'

Luzma stood and walked to the door.

'Where are you going?' Rafa asked jumping to his feet.

'I need some fresh air,' she said opening the door.

'I'll come with you,' he said.

'Rafa, leave me alone,' she said, her voice harsh.

He stared at her. She bit back her tears. Then she shut the door.

She walked in a daze to the secret storage space at the back of one of the classrooms where they had been sleeping. Rafa's bag, along with the spare clothes their friends had given them was in a drawer in the corner. Would he forgive her for taking his beloved camera? What other choice did she have? She needed the footage for her plan. She took the camera and replaced it with a quickly scribbled note.

Please forgive me, I will get your camera back to you, but I need to use the footage to get Jair back. I love you, but I don't want you to follow me. I don't want to see you again until I have Jair. Please leave and protect yourself.

She walked down the stairs, looking behind to make sure no-one was following her, and then walked outside. The rain pelted down. She moved faster down the driveway to the road, numb. Her mind screamed at her to turn back to the safety of Rafa and their friends, to do as they said and run as far away from this place as she possibly could. She stopped halfway down the driveway and turned to look back. Loneliness and fear tugged at her chest. She knew she had to keep going.

CHAPTER TWENTY-EIGHT

L uzma found it hard to think over the constant drum of the rain on the tin roofs around her. She used to find the sound soothing sitting on the porch back in Las Delicias watching the children play in the warm tropical storms, but not today. She pulled the cap she'd just bought further down over her face and looked around. Two kids played football in the street, their drenched hair clinging to the sides of their smiling faces. A group of women hung around the corner bakery chatting. The neighborhood seemed safe. But she doubted anywhere in Buenaventura was really secure for her anymore. It certainly wouldn't be after she made the call she was planning to make.

She carried a bag with the white dress and hat she had just bought with the money the nuns had given her. These were the traditional clothes being sold throughout the city. Everyone would be wearing a similar outfit for tomorrow night's Pacific Folkloric Music Festival. It should be easy to blend into the crowd and hide. At least that was what she was counting on.

The internet café across the road had only a few people inside and a teenage boy behind the counter who flirted with the girl in front of him. Everything seemed normal: no members of the army or anyone who was obviously from one of the groups. But one could never really tell.

She reached in her bag and picked up Rafa's camera. A mixture of guilt and sadness washed over her. She wished he was with her now. But she needed to protect him from what she was about to do. She turned it on and scrolled through the video files, as she had watched Rafa do many times, until she found what she was looking for. She pressed play and the recording of the General and El Cubano from the night in the factory began. She paused it at the part she wanted him to hear.

She knew her plan was desperate and highly risky. But the only other option was to go to them directly and beg them to let Jair go. Then she would definitely be killed, not to mention all the other things they would to do her. She shuddered. Her wet clothes clung to her skin. She had to try to keep the upper hand. At least, with this plan she was in control and she had some chance of saving Jair without getting herself killed.

Luzma's hands trembled as she turned the pages of the tattered directory. She found what she was looking for; the headquarters of the Armed Forces of Buenaventura. She put Rafa's camera before her, looking around. No-one seemed to be paying any attention but would they be able to overhear her conversation? The plastic booth was not exactly soundproof. The man at the desk was blasting American hip-hop from his computer so it was unlikely. She took a deep breath. This was what her mother would have done. She dialled the number.

'Army headquarters, Lieutenant Cosio speaking,' a man's voice said.

'Can I speak to General Ordonez?' she said slowly, suppressing the fear that was bubbling inside of her.

'And who can I say is speaking?' the man asked.

'Luz-Marina Cuesta.'

'I'll see if the General is available.'

After a long pause there was a rustling sound and then a voice.

'This is General Ordonez.'

Blood rushed to Luzma's head, and hatred and anger started to push the fear aside.

'This is Luz-Marina Cuesta. You and your friend El Cubano have my brother Jair.' Luzma's anger for what her brother might be suffering overtook her fear, bringing cold clarity to her thoughts. Her voice was calm.

'I don't know what you're talking about, Ms Cuesta, but I'd be happy to meet with you to discuss this with you.'

'I have something I want you to listen to.' She pressed Rafa's camera to the mouthpiece and pushed play.

El Cubano's voice could be heard. *'We can't let them wreck this plan. There are millions and millions of dollars at stake. We can retire with the amount of money we're going to get from this.'*

The General's distinctive voice cut in. *'I don't want to retire. I want to become the Army General, but if they find out that I'm working with you on this plan I'll not only lose my job, I'll be thrown in jail. No, we have to get rid of all these people who are jeopardizing the plan. I want that girl dead and her friend the American as well. We'll have to find a more creative way to get rid of him: a car accident on the way from Buenaventura to Cali perhaps. Those roads are so dangerous.'*

Luzma stopped the recording and let the silence sit.

'Did you hear all of that?' she asked.

'Where did you get that?' the General asked, any pretence of civility gone.

'It doesn't matter where I got it, but there's much more and video as well. I don't think the national government would be too pleased with this, nor would the US Embassy.' Fear had been completely replaced by rage and it was an oddly comforting emotion.

'What do you want?'

'My brother,' she replied. 'I will call you at 9am tomorrow morning with instructions of where you are to release him. If you fail to do so or if he or I or any of my friends are hurt, especially Rafael, this tape will be sent straight to the US Embassy, the national government and the media.'

'How do I know you haven't already shared it?'

'Because if I had, you would have been arrested by now,' Luzma said. 'General, make sure you have my brother with you and he is not harmed in any way tomorrow morning when I call you.' She hung up the phone.

She remembered Rafa's warning about the army tracing calls. She needed to get out of the area. She walked to the corner and hailed a passing minivan. The thought of spending a night alone in this city made her stomach churn. Nowhere was safe and she couldn't call anyone. She had committed to do this by herself. She thought of Jair and what he must be going through. She needed to be strong for him. It was only one more night and then, hopefully, they could be reunited and escape. But she knew the General and El Cubano were not going to give that to her easily.

CHAPTER TWENTY-NINE

'That little bitch!' General Ordonez screamed, slamming his mug down. Black coffee splashed across his desk and his one framed image fell over.

His phone rang.

He picked it up hurriedly. 'Did you trace the call?'

'Yes, sir. It came from Barrio Nueva Vida. But we don't have the exact address.'

'Get a small group together and get there immediately. I want that girl. Do you understand? I need her alive. I need to know what she's done with this information.'

'What information, sir?'

'Never mind, sergeant,' the General said. 'Just get me the girl. Keep it low profile, only the normal team.'

The muscles throughout his body tensed as they did every time he sensed the enemy was near. He picked up the photo that he had knocked over and grimaced at the crack that had formed in the glass. The thin line ran across his father's face. He gripped the photo frame with such ferocity that his arm began to shake. This girl was going to destroy everything he had worked for. He had dedicated twenty-four years of his life to ridding Colombia of guerrilla and other scum and now all his sacrifices could be for nothing if the national government got a hold of that video.

He was not the only one to take advantage of the drug money; throughout his career he had seen nearly all of his superiors do it. How else was a man supposed to live and support his family and mistresses on these pathetic wages? Why should the guerrilla and the paramilitaries be the only ones to benefit? Maybe he had taken it too far by supporting this submarine idea. It had seemed particularly risky. But the money was so enticing, and plus, he controlled this town and he could make sure no-one found out. Well, that was what he had thought. If his superiors found out about this his career was over. He would never make Army General.

He looked down at the photo of his father and was filled with sadness. He wanted to proudly follow his father's footsteps to lead his country's armed forces, but if he didn't stop this girl that would never happen. Even worse, he could end up extradited on drug charges to some maximum security jail in the US where he would share a cell full of *maricas*.

What if the girl was lying and she had already given the footage to the authorities? Surely if that was the case they would have come for him already, as she had said. He couldn't be certain. They had to get this submarine into the water straightaway. He could make his millions on that first shipment and then shut down the operation. Taking a breath, he calmly picked up the phone and dialled.

CHAPTER THIRTY

'Who chose this place? I don't like it,' Nathaniel said, scanning the area. It was like a graveyard for the containers that were no longer in use at the port. He took in the small gaps between the containers, like miniature alleyways. The tops of the crates were out of sight and long shadows were cast by the setting sun.

'He suggested it,' Jose said. 'He said it was isolated so it would be easier to talk here.'

'Mauricio, good to see you,' Nathaniel said, extending a hand as they reached the young man. Mauricio's hand was clammy, his grip weak. 'So what's the matter? Has something happened?'

Mauricio looked around, blinking as the rain ran into his eyes.

'They're onto me. I'm certain they know. You have to get me out of here.'

Nathaniel glanced at Jose. 'What makes you think that?'

'They're always watching me, even when I leave. You have to help me get out of here.' Mauricio's words scrambled together; fast and breathless.

Nathaniel surveyed the area. 'Are you sure you weren't followed today?'

Mauricio's eyes widened as he looked around. 'I don't think so.'

Jose touched his arm, holding him still. 'Mauricio, tell us exactly what's happened. The more exact you can be the better able we are to help you.'

'I feel like I'm being watched all the time. I think they know about the tracking device.'

'You know, most people wouldn't have a clue what the device was if they saw it. To the average person it appears like a simple small battery,' Nathaniel said. 'Are you sure you're not just imagining this.'

'No,' Mauricio snapped. 'Ever since then I've seen them watching me, they even spy on me when I'm at home.'

The rain intensified, drumming insistently against the crates.

'Should we go to the car and talk about it there?' Jose shouted over the racket.

'Only if you're going to get Diana and me out of here now, otherwise, I can't risk being seen with you.'

'Where are they up to with the submarine?' Nathaniel asked.

'The welding, pneumatics and electrics are finished. Now it's just testing and fine tuning. We should be ready to start sea trials in a day or two.'

'So how long do you think it will take them to be ready to launch it with the drugs onboard?'

Mauricio wiped the rain from his face. 'I don't know. If they continue to work us around the clock like dogs then I suppose in less than a week.'

Nathaniel let out a low whistle. 'That's soon.'

'Look please, you have to help me,' Mauricio begged. 'If you don't get me out of here I won't be alive in a week.'

'The problem is if you just suddenly go missing then they're really going to be suspicious and the last thing we can afford right now is to spook them,' Jose said.

'Haven't you been listening to me?' Mauricio shouted. 'I'm going to be killed if you don't get me out. Remember I'm in this situation because of you.'

'We understand that Mauricio.' Nathaniel held up a hand. 'Your safety is also our priority. We need to think of how we can get you out without spooking El Cubano's men. When is your next day off?'

'I don't have days off. They let me have Sunday morning off to go to the church and that's it.'

Nathaniel was torn. He didn't want to risk Mauricio's life. They were responsible for his safety. But he also couldn't afford to blow the operation. As far as he was aware, El Cubano knew nothing about them. But if one of the workers in the factory disappeared without warning it would raise suspicion.

'Look, Mauricio, you'll have to give us a couple of days. We have to come up with a story El Cubano would believe and logistics around it. We also need to find a safe house for you and your family in Bogota before you go to the US.'

'I don't know. How long will you take? I don't want to die. I want to see my family again.'

Nathaniel cringed.

'You will see your family,' he said. 'We will have you out of here by the weekend.'

'What about Diana? If I'm in danger so is she. We both need to leave.'

'We will get a message to you by Friday with the plan and if something happens in the meantime, you call me straightaway,' Nathaniel said.

'Promise you won't leave me any longer.'

'I promise.' Nathaniel didn't like himself as he said the words. He felt like a slimy politician telling Mauricio what he wanted to hear. But what choice did he have? This operation was too important. He couldn't risk stuffing it up now. They had come too far.

Nathaniel's phone rang as he and Jose walked back to the car.

'Nat, it's Peter.' The DEA's communication specialist was calling. He was based in a team in Bogota that monitored all the DEA targets' phones.

El Cubano and the General's mobile phones were on the list so he contacted Nat when he heard something of interest, which was not often. El Cubano was obviously wary of talking on the phone so most of the time what Peter heard was the paramilitary boss boasting about his most recent conquest: entertaining to start with, but not of great use to the mission. However, this very technology had helped them in countless other operations. It just required patience.

'Tell me,' Nathaniel said.

'Pablo Ruiz just got a call originating from the military base. I haven't checked it with our voice recognition gear, but I think it was General Ordonez on the other end of the line.'

'What did he say?'

'The person I believe to be the General said time had run out and that they needed to fast-track things before it was too late. Pablo told him they shouldn't speak on the phone and suggested that they meet in person.'

'When and where are they meeting?'

'They didn't specify where. They just said the normal place in two hours,' Jairo replied.

'Anything else?'

'No, that's it.'

'Excellent work. Let me know as soon as you get a confirmation on the caller.' Nathaniel hung up.

CHAPTER THIRTY-ONE

The General looked out the blackened bulletproof window at the pulsing streets of central Buenaventura. Only a night before the Pacific Folkloric Music Festival people were gearing into carnival mode. He would like to be so oblivious to reality, to be lost with his lover in a night of sex and alcohol. He would like to be meeting her instead of having to meet Pablo Ruiz. But he did not have the luxury of innocence like civilians did. Right now he had to prevent this meddling bitch from destroying his whole career, his whole life.

The car moved past the packed main square where people crowded around makeshift food stands and bars. Bars pumped out an eclectic mix of American hip-hop and traditional Colombian music. A couple walked in front of the General's car, paying little attention, too intoxicated by eachother to notice. The music softened a few notches as the car rounded the corner and headed down a side street, stopping at the very end of the road. The General exited the vehicle, looking around cautiously.

'Gilberto, you stay with the car,' he said to the driver. 'We'll be back soon.'

The General and two of his sergeants walked down the jetty at the end of the road, where an army speedboat awaited them. The skipper revved the engine and the smell of gasoline filled the air. The crew released the ropes, reversed and then threw the boat into drive, the water flying up around them as they shot forward. The night was black with only a sliver of the moon visible. They flew across the water for ten minutes before reaching the island. The strobe light highlighted a solitary boat moored at the jetty.

'That's unusual. He's on time for once. I wonder if that's a good sign or a bad one,' the General wondered.

They cut the engine and slid the boat into the jetty in front of the other speedboat. One of the men jumped off and tied the ropes to the bollards. Two men with AK-47s watched them silently.

'Where's Pablo?' the General asked from the boat. He could not see him, but he knew Ruiz was around by the heavy smell of cigar that hung in the air.

'I'm here, my friend, waiting for you,' Pablo Ruiz said, climbing out of the saloon onto the jetty, the trademark cigar wedged between his lips. He took the General's hand and gave him a friendly slap on the back.

The General forced a smile, masking the disdain he felt in Pablo's presence.

Pablo took a torch from one of his men and shone it down to the end of the wharf where two seats were set up.

'I thought that would be a nice place for a talk.' He looked back to his men on the boat. Three of you and one of the General's men take a boat and patrol the area to make sure no-one is around. The other boat stays on guard here.'

Together they walked down the jetty and sat in the low chairs by the water. Pablo shone the torch beside him and pulled up a bottle of *aguadiente* and two plastic glasses. He poured the General a glass and handed it to him, then poured himself one and let the torch sit on the wharf, creating a narrow tunnel of light in the water before them.

'Salud,' Pablo said as he threw back a large swig of the potent liquid.

The General grimaced. *Aguadiente* was such a peasant drink and he hated the overpowering smell and taste of aniseed. But for now, he thought it best to be polite and sipped a small amount of the liquid, which left his mouth and lips burning.

'So what's this situation we have?' Pablo asked.

The General took another sip of the drink. He needed something to numb him. 'That girl and the American are going to cause us even more trouble than we'd imagined,' he said.

'You mean the same girl who went to the local authorities with what her brother overheard?'

'That's the one,' the General said, gripping the glass so tightly that the plastic cracked, spilling the remaining liquid over his hand.

'That little bitch is going to be the end of me.'

'What do you mean?'

'It seems they somehow sneaked into the factory and have footage of you and me talking about the plan.'

'What?' Pablo asked. 'That's impossible. We have that area covered in security.'

'That's what I thought as well. But she played me the recording and sure as hell it's you and me talking about what we should do with the boy and killing her and the American.'

'Has she given it to the authorities? What's she planning on doing with it?' Pablo had turned to face him, one hand on the edge of his chair.

'She says she hasn't. She says she'll give us the video if we return her brother. I hope you haven't killed him yet,' the General said, looking over at Pablo. He could just see the faint outline of the man's chubby face from the light that filtered up from the torch.

'No, I haven't killed him. We agreed we'd keep him as bait until we get the girl. But we can't trust her. How do we know she hasn't already given it to the authorities?' His usual long drawl had gone now, his voice sounded slightly frayed.

'Of course, we can't trust her. However, if she's already given the recording to the authorities surely we'd know about it by now.'

'You'd assume so, but you never know what they're up to. We have to get this girl so we can know exactly what she's done and who else has a copy,' Pablo said.

'I agree, but she's proving harder to catch than I would have imagined. She called me today and I had the call traced and men sent to the area, but they didn't find her. I've had men out searching for her all day and we haven't found anything.'

'You should have let me know,' Pablo said. 'My men could have found her.'

'What do you think? You've got better intelligence than the Colombian Army?' the General said, not hiding his annoyance.

'It doesn't matter who is better. The point is we both could have been looking for her.'

The General hated talking to this arrogant half-breed, but he had too much at stake to let his ego get in the way. He hoped to be free of this man once the deliveries had been made.

'She said she would call at nine tomorrow morning to tell me where she wants the boy to be released. If we can't get her beforehand then both your men and mine can make sure we pick her and her friend up at the drop-off. I've also got someone working on a case against her and the American. He's collecting some evidence linking them to drug smuggling and the guerrilla so they will be discredited. For now, I want to get this submarine out of here in case she does share the video and the national government and their American allies turn up.'

'I agree. If the shipment is captured I'm a dead man. But when I talked to the head Russian engineer yesterday he said he probably needed at least five days to finish it, do some trials in the water and strengthen the old slipway.'

'Screw the tests. We don't have time for that. We should assume the worst: that the national authorities and their *gringo* buddies could arrive any time now and we need to make sure the submarine is gone. I think we should move it tonight.'

'Impossible!' Pablo said. 'Even without the trials it will take several days still. And that's pushing it.'

'Well, we need to push it. Talk to the engineers and see if you can't get it in the water sooner,' the General said.

'Look, we have sources everywhere. We'd know if they were going to raid it. But fine, I'll talk to the head engineer when I get back to see when the earliest possible launch date could be.'

'What about the drugs?' the General asked. 'You can't load them in the factory. We need them out of there just in case it's raided.'

'And where would you suggest we load them then?' Pablo asked

'This is a submarine, you know, not a little speedboat. We can't just load it anywhere.'

'I'm sure you can think of a place. There are hundreds of inlets where you could easily load without being seen,' the General said impatiently.

'Well, I can't organize it tonight. It's too complicated for that. I can have them moved from the laboratory to a pick-up point tomorrow but I'll need you to ensure the coastguard or the rest of the armed forces don't get in our way.'

'Tell me what route you'll take and I'll have someone listen to all communications to make sure no-one is patrolling that area and let you know if you need to deviate the path at all.'

'Good. I'll have a message sent to you tomorrow with the plan and with a secure number your men can reach us on if we need to change things.'

'If all goes as planned the drugs will be taken to a separate location, the submarine will be launched within a day or two and, hopefully, we can capture the girl and the American tomorrow and find out who they've shared the video with,' the General said, wrapping up the conversation. He didn't want to speak to this man any more than was necessary.

'Let us know where she is and we'll make sure we get her,' Pablo said. 'We're very good at that.'

CHAPTER THIRTY-TWO

'I want to help you, but you're going to have to be clear on what's going on,' Nathaniel said.

Luzma looked around her. The street was empty apart from the woman whose phone she was using and a gaggle of kids heading to school.

'I don't have a lot of time. I'll tell you later. I need your help tonight.'

'If you're planning something I need to know what it is. We have an operation at stake.' His voice was stern.

Blood rushed to Luzma's face and when she spoke her voice sounded harsher than she had intended. 'Well, my brother's life is at stake. You wouldn't have an operation if we hadn't given you that information and footage. Now I need your help.'

'What do you have in mind?' Nathaniel asked.

'Can we meet at 9.30pm at *Casa del Sol*? And can you get Rafa out of Buenaventura before then?'

The woman behind the cart stared at her. Luzma tried to move farther away, but the phone was attached by a cord. She crouched down beside the cart and angled her body away from the woman. Anyone in this city could be a spy for the paramilitaries.

'9.30 is too late. We already have a trip to Cali planned tonight and we can't wait that long. But, if you can meet us by 7.30 at the latest we'll find a way to take you with us.'

'You can't make it any later?'

'No.'

That would mean that she would have to ask the General to release Jair at 7.00. It was not ideal. The best bands came on later so the crowd would not be as full and there would still be traces of sunlight. It would not be as easy to hide. But, she needed the Americans' help. If she and Jair could get to them, they would be safe.

'Okay, we'll meet you at 7.30pm at *Casa del Sol*. You will definitely be there, right?'

'We will be there.'

'Do you promise?'

There was an uncomfortable pause that filled the space with doubt.

'We'll be there.'

Luzma hung up. The street was quiet apart from the rustling as she toyed with the pieces of paper in her hand. The first call was the easy one.

A man with shoulder-length plaits was opening a small barber shop on the corner and further down the street a woman was hanging bunches of small bananas in front of her store. Everything looked normal. But one could never be sure in Buenaventura.

She took a deep breath and tried to feel the presence of God and her ancestors inside her. She had played this plan over and over in her mind last night. Her mind was the most powerful thing she had after her connection to God, Grandma had always told her. Control it and she could have anything she wanted.

She pictured Jair's arms wrapped around her waist as she dialled the number. A man answered the phone.

'The General, please,' she said. 'I'm in a hurry.'

She glanced at her watch. The seconds ticked by. A car engine rumbled. She turned her hunched back to the road. Her breath grew faster as time passed. The car drove down the road and continued. Where was he? The general was so used to controlling everything and treating people like the dust under his boots. He thought he would just silence her like he had done to everyone else who got in his way, but she would make sure he and El Cubano and

165

their men were brought to justice for everything they had done. Firstly, she needed to get Jair back.

'Miss Cuesta.'

'Do you have my brother?'

'No.'

The word felt like a punch to her gut.

There was a long pause. 'But I can get him.'

She let out her breath slowly, steadying herself. 'Tonight at 7pm release him by the lighthouse in the middle of the park during the festival.'

'That will be a bit busy, don't you think? You might never find him. I'm sure we can find a better place.' His words were slow and measured.

'No. Tonight at 7pm at the lighthouse or I will send the video to the Embassy and the national authorities.' The adrenaline that pumped through her body washed away any thoughts or doubts.

'Well, maybe we can figure something out,' he said slowly.

'Yes or no? Tell me now or I send the video. No maybe.'

'How do I know you won't just send the video once I've released him?'

'Someone will be there to give you the video as soon as you have released him,' she said, bluffing.

'And how do I know you haven't made copies?'

'Look, all I care about is my brother. You release him and leave us alone and I'll give you the video back and will leave you alone. Do we have a deal?'

'Fine.'

'Good. Release him at 7pm at the lighthouse and you will be given the video. If I see anyone else there, I'll send the video to the authorities.'

As Luzma hung up she pushed away the fear in her gut, the fear warning her that this plan was going to go terribly wrong.

CHAPTER THIRTY-THREE

El Cubano flung open the doors from his bedroom to the balcony.

'If you're waking me up this early, this better be good,' he said gruffly.

The teenager standing before him squirmed. His limbs appeared childlike under the canopy of his clothes.

'I think you will want to hear this, sir,' he said quietly.

Pablo grunted. 'So why are you here at 8am on a Saturday morning?'

'I tried to tell you last night, sir,' the young man said, 'but I was told you were at an important meeting. I waited over an hour but you didn't return so I thought I ought to get back to following the electrician. I just clocked off my shift and came straight here.'

'What exactly is it you wanted to tell me?'

'The electrician is a traitor, sir.'

'What do you mean?' Pablo asked, suddenly feeling very awake.

'I've been following him around. Yesterday, late afternoon after he finished work he caught a van out of town. He was all fidgety, looking around, couldn't keep still. I thought he's either on crack or he's up to something. I kept my distance, like they do in the movies. I saw him get off just out of town where they store all the old shipping containers. I crept around the containers until I found him there by himself in the middle. He was shaking like a girl. So I climbed up to the top of the containers to lie there and wait.'

'What happened?' Pablo asked.

'Well, I waited for a while and then two other people showed up. I couldn't see them, but just heard their voices. One sounded like he was from the countryside or another state. But the other one had to be a foreigner. He spoke real strange.'

'Where was he from?' Pablo interjected. 'Was he American?'

'I don't know any people from other countries so I can't say. He sounded a bit like a robot and his Spanish was worse than my kid brother's.'

'It's got to be the *gringos*,' Pablo said. 'So what did they say?'

'It was hard to hear because it started to rain really hard. The electrician was nervous and kept telling the others that they needed to get him out of Buenaventura and that he was being watched which I thought was kinda funny.' The teenager laughed at his own joke.

'What else? Tell me exactly what they said,' Pablo demanded impatiently.

'He was talking about the submarine and kept on begging them to help him get out of Buenaventura. He said we knew what he was doing and he also mentioned something about a device.'

'A device?' Pablo asked. 'What sort of device?'

'I don't know, sorry. Like I said, it was raining like crazy and I couldn't hear everything. I just heard him say device, but I don't know anything else.'

'And when did this happen?'

'Yesterday evening, sir. But like I said, I tried to tell you but you were at a meeting and I didn't want to leave the electrician for too long.'

'Why didn't you call me?'

'You told me and the others never to call you about important business. You said we couldn't trust the phone lines.'

'I want to speak to the electrician now. Bring that little *sapo* to the centre immediately. By the time I'm finished with him he'll tell us every detail of what he's been up to and will regret the day he ever spoke to the gringos.'

Mauricio's body writhed in the frantic movement that came with the knowledge that death was near. El Cubano had seen it many times before. He enjoyed holding the power over someone's life.

El Cubano slowly opened a bag, pulling out an electric drill and holding it before Mauricio like a present. The man's bruised eyes widened. El Cubano plugged the device in, his movements slow and deliberate.

'I'm not an expert in this machine,' he said. 'But I'm sure I can learn. I might make some mistakes, of course.'

The machine revved to life. El Cubano brought the drill close to Mauricio's face. The young man's chin trembled.

'Would you prefer somewhere else to begin with?' El Cubano brought the tip of the machine above Mauricio's hand.

'No, please don't,' Maurcio begged, shaking his head. Then he let out a cry like a wild animal as El Cubano pushed the drill into his hand that was bound to the side of the chair. The young man's head slumped to his chin.

Pablo rolled his eyes. 'That didn't take long. Wake him up with some water. I'm sure he'll be ready to talk now.'

One of Pablo's men threw a bucket of cold water over Mauricio's head. The electrician gasped. He looked down at his hand and vomited.

'Stop being so pathetic,' El Cubano shouted at him. 'You either tell me exactly what you're doing with the gringos, or it will be your dick next, if I can find it, that is. Take off his pants,' he ordered one of his men.

'No, please, no. I'll tell you everything. Please just stop.'

'Everything?' El Cubano asked, bending over so his face was in line with Mauricio's. 'The pain you have felt so far is nothing compared to what you'll feel if you lie to me. Not to mention what I'll do to your family.'

Mauricio's eyes watered and he began to speak. 'There are two of them. They told me they were from the US Government and that they knew I was working with you and that we were building a submarine in the factory to export drugs to the United States.'

Mauricio's voice trembled. 'They said they had proof I was working with you and that they would send me to prison in the US for a long time if I didn't help them.'

'How would they know we were building a submarine in the factory?' El Cubano asked.

'I don't know. But when they came to me they knew more than I did. I was never told what it was for.'

'The girl's video that the General mentioned,' Carlos said. He stood in the corner, almost unnoticeable. 'She must have already shared it with the authorities.'

El Cubano turned to face him, gripping the drill like a gun. 'I am going to find that fucking whore and she is going to pay.' He turned to Mauricio. 'So what did you do for them?'

'They told me if I didn't help them I would rot in an American jail.'

'I don't give a fuck what they told you. What did you do for them?'

'They made me put a tracking device on the submarine.' Mauricio's voice was high-pitched, desperate.

There was a pause as the words sunk in and then El Cubano drove his fist hard into Mauricio's cheek. The man's head whipped back and the entire chair toppled, the back of his skull smashing against the concrete floor.

'You piece of shit!' El Cubano screamed, kicking Mauricio's chest and head.

'Stop! I can remove it for you. Please stop.'

'He's right,' Carlos said. 'We need him alive to find and get rid of this device. If you kill him how are we going to find it?'

El Cubano launched a final kick into Mauricio's ribs. Then he turned his back and walked away. 'Get this traitor together and bring him to the factory. And make sure no-one sees you. We can't let them know he's been caught.' As he was stepping through the door he called over his shoulder, 'and find that little bitch. I want the pleasure of killing her.'

170

CHAPTER THIRTY-FOUR

El Cubano strode into the factory. Behind him Carlos dragged Mauricio by the collar. He shuffled limply, bound and gagged. El Cubano stopped in the middle of the factory, his body tense and ready to throw a punch. The men working on the submarine watched him out of the corner of their eyes, busying themselves with their work.

'Where is it?' El Cubano asked, ripping the old rag out of Maurcio's mouth.

He coughed and gulped in air, his chest heaving. Then he stared mutely at the submarine.

El Cubano pulled out his handgun and held it to Mauricio's forehead.

'It's in the control room,' Mauricio said, his voice barely audible.

'Where exactly?'

'In the junction box closest to the conning tower.'

'Petrov,' El Cubano said, addressing the head engineer. 'Can you figure out how we can get rid of this tracking device without the gringos realising?'

The tall Russian nodded. 'Let's locate it first and I'll find a way.'

'Now, you listen carefully,' El Cubano said, circling Mauricio.

'You are going to show us exactly where it is. If you try to pull any tricks your mother and those pretty sisters of yours will die.'

Tears rolled down Mauricio's face.

'Stop being such a girl and tell me you understand,' El Cubano said.

Everyone in the room stared. Mauricio nodded.

'If you only move the device a small distance they won't pick it up, especially if you move it directly up or down,' the engineer said. 'We could take it out through the conning tower above us and place it on the rafters directly above the submarine. That way it shouldn't register any movement.'

'But, this little son of a bitch hasn't just hidden it on the submarine,' El Cubano said, barely able to control his anger. 'He's wired it into the control room. Won't they notice if that wiring is broken?'

'It's obviously operating from its own battery pack at the moment because the submarine hasn't been powered up.' The Russian pointed to the back of the small device. 'So they won't notice if it's unwired.'

'Get it out,' El Cubano said. 'Then we launch at nightfall so we can be well on our way before they have a chance to get suspicious.'

'I can launch it tonight, but it won't leave the wharf for twenty-four hours,' Petrov said.

'You don't have twenty-four hours. I need this underwater before the gringos realise their tracking device is no longer onboard.'

'This is a submarine, not a fishing boat.'

Heat rushed to El Cubano's face. 'What do you think I am, an idiot? People who speak to me like that don't last long.'

The engineer paused. 'I'm sorry, but I told you from the beginning that we needed at least twenty-four hours to do sea trials. It's impossible just to launch it and be on your way. This is a complex vessel.'

'I understand that, but you need to understand the situation we're in. Thanks to this little traitor, the gringos could be here at any moment. I need to get this into the water, pick up the drugs tonight and be on the way to the US before they realise what has happened.'

'Yes, but as I have explained from the start, once the submarine is in the water we need to check the pumping, hydraulic and high pressure systems and run the air compressors. We also need to run the diesel engines and throw the main DC circuit breaker and double check the connection to all the sub's electrical circuits to the batteries. Without that we're not moving anywhere.'

El Cubano tried to interrupt him, but the Russian held up his hand and continued.

'Then we need to check the trim of the submarine and its draft to make sure it will dive as planned then do a static dive beside the wharf. Then and only then will we be ready to move her.'

El Cubano wondered why on earth he had not stuck to trafficking routes and methods he knew well. From the start he could barely understand any of the technicalities Petrov and his team mentioned. That put him in the vulnerable position of having to listen to them. He hated that.

'Fine. We launch at sunset, you run the trials and then we pick up the drugs at 4.30 am. That gives you more than ten hours to get it all done.'

'It's not enough time,' Petrov protested.

'It will have to be. You can have as many men as you need to help you. But there is no more time.'

CHAPTER THIRTY-FIVE

Luzma was alone in a sea of strangers. Eyes peered down at her from all directions. Any one of them could belong to one of El Cubano or the General's men. Maybe the man to her right, whose eyes lingered on her for a little too long, or the boy who seemed to trail behind her. Feet pounded the earth to the sound of the *tambores*. She tried to concentrate, but the noise was all consuming. The rhythm of the drums thumped in her chest.

She was sure the General and El Cubano would have men positioned all around the park. They wanted the tape, so hopefully they would go along with her plan and bring Jair. They wouldn't let her go easily. The plan teetered on insanity. But she had no choice. She had to walk along a cliff's edge, hoping she wouldn't fall.

Head down, she pushed against the wave of people. She needed to reach one of the elevated viewing platforms that had been erected around the park. From there she would be able to see the place where the General was to release Jair, and she could try to put her plan into motion.

'What's the rush, honey?' a man's voice said from above her, grabbing her hand and pulling her back. 'Let's dance.'

She yanked her hand away and pushed harder against the crowd, shoulders hunched. She finally reached the stairs to the side of the stage. Stepping up she surveyed the crowd. She squinted, trying to make out faces among the pulsating mass of color and skin. The mini lighthouse in the middle of the park was lit up, precisely why she had asked the General to meet there. But he wasn't there yet. It was only 6.30pm.

Suddenly a face stood out from the crowd. She recognized the paramilitary officer who had stopped her the day she had met Rafa. He had the same cap sitting high on his shaven head. He was only ten meters away to her right. There were two other men with him and they weren't dancing. They were clearly prowling around looking for her. On the rafter she was exposed. She needed to hide. A group of women carrying colorful dresses walked past her to the left, heading for the change room. She jumped down and let herself be swept up by the group.

The smell of perfume was overpowering in the cramped change room. The women laughed and shouted at each other over the beat of the music. Luzma looked through the curtains.

The paramilitary men were only five metres away now. She stepped back.

'Ouch, watch out!' one woman said.

'Sorry,' Luzma said, backing away from the curtains.

'If you've finished getting dressed you can leave to make room for the rest of us,' the woman said.

Luzma shook her head. Had they seen her? Were they waiting for her? If she left now they would catch her for sure and then what use would she be to Jair? She unzipped her dress and fiddled with her bra and zipper to look like she belonged.

Women came and went, readying themselves for their performance. Some of them looked at Luzma strangely, others seemed to not notice her in the corner. The drums began to pulse louder accompanied by the melody of the marimba. The sound reminded Luzma of the jungle and of home. She promised herself that she would get Jair and take him back there.

She glanced at her watch. It was 6.50pm. Only ten minutes to go. It was relatively empty in the change room now, with just two other women who wore rainbow skirts and flowers in their hair. Luzma edged to the curtain door and looked out. Performers bustled around, waiting to go on stage. The men were nowhere to be seen. She left the little room and joined the group of performers to the side of the stage.

The band began to sing 'Mi Buenaventura' and the audience erupted. The people around Luzma began to move, skirts swishing, white handkerchiefs twirling, men grinning as they circled the women. The song reminded Luzma of Jair and of afternoons dancing around the house together, teasing their grandparents until finally they relented and joined in. She wished she could be there in the kitchen in Las Delicias dancing with her family. Instead she was here, trying to save her brother's life.

It was 7pm; time to see if the General had arrived. She pushed her way back to the stairs, her gaze darting in every direction. Stepping up onto the ledge, she held her breath, hoping she would see Jair. But there was no sign of him or the General.

The next thirty minutes were torture. She checked her watch incessantly. All she could do was stare at the lighthouse and then at her watch. Had the general changed his mind? Had the plan backfired? Was Jair alive? The thought made her nauseous.

'Dear God, please protect Jair and bring him to me,' she whispered. But she couldn't even hear her own words over the top of the pounding music.

At 7.45pm her stomach dropped. Her mind had been whirling through possible explanations why they hadn't arrived yet. Voices chattered in her head as loud as the music on stage. She searched the crowd desperately for a sign of him, but found nothing. And then a premonition came to her as clear as they always were.

Luzma pushed blindly through the crowd. She needed to get to *Casa del Sol* before the Americans left. She had to convince them to help her get Jair. Otherwise, she would have to confront El Cubano by herself and that would mean death.

She finally broke through the crowd and ran across the road, barely bothering to look around. *Casa del Sol* was only four blocks away. The back streets would be faster so she bolted down an alleyway. She crossed onto the second block, holding her skirt in bunches to avoid falling.

'Luz-Marina,' a man's voice called from behind.

She spun around. The paramilitary officer she had seen earlier stood a block away, pointing a gun at her head. She bolted around the corner, leaving him swearing behind her. The street was dark and her sandals slipped on the garbage-strewn ground. She lurched forward, reaching for the wall to steady herself, but missed, thudding to her knees. The man was behind her screaming for her to stop. She managed to scramble to her feet and sprinted away. The man's feet pounded the ground just metres from her. She skidded around the next corner, heading back towards the festival.

Suddenly a car pulled out in front of her, blocking her path. She turned. The man was just behind her. She tried to get past the car, but the door opened, blocking her path. The man grabbed her shoulder and spun her around. He shoved her hard against the wall.

'Where the fuck do you think you're going?' He put the muzzle of the gun to her forehead.

CHAPTER THIRTY-SIX

The air in the house smelt of filth as Luzma inhaled short, shallow breaths. The light from the television screen flickered across the men's faces, highlighting eyes that raked over her body. She tried to turn around but a pack of them had surrounded her.

'Please let me go,' she said. 'I have the recording from the factory that you want.'

'You are what we want,' the tall bald man said, his breath hot on her cheek. He grabbed the sleeves of her dress and yanked it down. The cotton tore and his fingers ripped at her flesh. More hands pulled at the dress. Luzma tried to hold onto it and cover herself, but more hands grabbed her wrists and yanked them behind her back.

A sickening feeling of utter vulnerability spread throughout her body. It was the same sensation she had experienced ten years ago. The same feeling she had tried to suppress all these years. Her body was limp, exposed, a plaything for them to use however they wished.

'Let me go.'

Their voices, laughing and jeering, were mixed with the sound of the television where bombs exploded and guns fired.

'Oh, we've only just begun,' one man said.

God, please help me. Please don't let them hurt me. But she couldn't feel even a glimmer of God in this hellhole.

One man pushed forward, a bottle of rum in his hand. He rubbed his body against her; the smell of the stale alcohol and tobacco was overwhelming. Nausea surged through her, and she vomited all over him. There was a pause and then laughter, more jeering and then the pain. His fist planted into her cheek so hard that she reeled backwards and blacked out.

When she came to moments later the disgusting man covered in her vomit stood over her. He reached down to pull up her dress and the bottle of rum in his hand slipped and fell on her lap, pouring its dark liquid over the white dress. The déjà vu was sickening. She remembered sitting on the stairs in front of their house ten years ago after the paramilitary officer climbed off her and looking down at the red stain that had seeped across her new white dress.

'Jair,' she said. At least don't let this be for nothing.

'Please kill me but let Jair go.'

The man above her was beginning to undo his trousers. Where would he keep his gun? Maybe she could kill just one of them before they could stop her. Then they would probably shoot her, but she would prefer that. At least then she could avoid the suffering.

The tall skinny man pushed the other man aside. 'Wait. Pablo has been after this one for ages. Let's call him first.'

El Cubano? Just the sound of his name was like a spotlight magnifying the fear and repulsion she felt.

'Boss, you'll never believe who we have here,' the man above her said and then responding to something El Cubano said he continued. 'Yeah, don't worry Boss, Marco and I are leaving for Bezan in the next half an hour. It will take us less than an hour to get there so we have plenty of time to get the merchandise ready for the 4.30am transfer. But don't you want to hear who we have? You're going to be very happy.'

Luzma couldn't breathe. Her head was spinning. *Please don't let El Cubano come.*

'The girl. The one who made the video that nearly wrecked everything and who told on us with that little muttering idiot brother of hers.'

'I knew you'd be happy. Yeah, I'll get her ready for you.'

'Please let Jair and I go.' The voice coming from her own mouth was someone else's, a child perhaps.

'Shut up, you stupid bitch,' the man above her said as he put his boot into her face, covering her mouth and pushing the sole of his shoe into her cheek so hard that she felt like her head might explode.

'You have a very special visitor coming,' he said.

She tried to scream, but he drove the boot further into her face. Pain pumped through her head as the pressure grew and then she blacked out again.

CHAPTER THIRTY-SEVEN

'I want the submarine in the water now!' El Cubano shouted.
'We have a 4.30am pick-up at Bezan and you can't be late.'

The factory felt like a sauna with the day's hot air trapped under the tin roof. Sweat dripped down El Cubano's back. He needed to get this into the water before the US authorities realised their tracking device was no longer where it should be.

'Everybody take your stations and do final checks. We launch in five minutes,' Petrov called out to his workers.

The tension was as stifling as the air. The submarine was held up by a large steel cradle that held its hundred-ton weight. The Russians ran around checking the twenty small steel wheels that spread the weight of the cradle onto the rail that ran down the slipway.

'Do you think this will work?' El Cubano asked Carlos, who stood beside him.

'The Russians say the weight of the sub is spread over the entire cradle and they can just ease it down the slipway,' Carlos said, looking up at the submarine.

'You make it sound very easy.'

'Well, it has to work, doesn't it? We don't have another option,' Carlos said.

El Cubano lit another cigar. 'As far as we know they might have detected that the tracking device was moved, they'll come to check sooner or later.'

'Surely they would have been here by now if they knew,' Carlos said, glancing sideways at El Cubano.

'You'd think so. But I will be much happier when this is in the water and even more so once the coke is loaded and it's on its way to LA.'

'They're ready for her there?'

'I called the contact today to tell him we're moving things forward. He whined like a bitch, but agreed in the end.'

The stern of the submarine was pointing towards the open doors leading to the river. From the ground looking up it appeared to El Cubano as if the conning tower would touch the factory's overhead beams.

The cradle groaned as the winch holding it in place was slowly released. The submarine seemed to rock slightly as it was eased backwards.

'Gentle,' Petrov said to the man controlling the electric winch.

The skipper and two of his men stood on the deck ready to tie the submarine up to the wharf as soon as it was launched. The submarine shook and rumbled as it picked up speed on its short journey to the water.

El Cubano stepped outside, surveying the area. It was pitch dark apart from the inkling of light reflecting off the water from the sliver of moon. He cocked his left ear to the sky. He expected to hear the sounds of a chopper or speedboat approaching, but there was silence apart from the scraping of the wheels against the reinforced steel tracks.

The submarine picked up speed as it reached the slipway leading to the water. Standing to the left, El Cubano began to smile as the submarine slid closer to the water. But then all of a sudden there was a loud groan and the submarine shuddered to a halt, rocking from side to side. There was a collective gasp as everyone looked on.

'What's wrong? Get this thing moving,' El Cubano said, looking at his men.

Everyone stared mutely at the submarine.

'Fix it. I want this in the water now!' El Cubano shouted at Petrov. The last thing he could afford was for the submarine to be stuck outside, exposed. He grabbed one of the guards who stood back at the corner watching. 'Circle the area and radio the cars at the entrance and the boats up river to make sure they haven't seen anything. I want to know if they're coming for us.'

'Yes, sir.'

'Bring the spotlights down to the water's edge,' Petrov said. He waded up to his knees in water, shining a torch at the slipway. 'One of the steel beams has buckled under the sub's weight. The only hope we have is to use the big jacks and pray we can force it back into position.'

The workers ran into the factory to collect the jacks and the timber to position them as Petrov instructed. With all three in place they began.

'Slowly. We've got a hundred-ton sub above us,' Petrov said, standing beside the men as they pumped and applied a load to the jacks.

El Cubano paced back and forth, unable to do anything.

Petrov stepped back and looked along the length of the main rail. 'It can't be much more, it looks close.'

Suddenly the cradle creaked and made a jerk as it moved forward and took up the slack on the winch. The men scrambled out of the way and El Cubano let out a sigh.

'Ease her forward gently,' Petrov called out.

Everyone stared silently as the submarine moved forward, swaying from side to side. Finally the submarine made it to the water and then floated free of the cradle. The skipper started both diesel engines and the submarine came to life. El Cubano punched the air in victory and everyone cheered. The skipper manoeuvred the submarine the short distance to the end of the wharf that ran out from the factory and his men tied it up.

'Petrov,' El Cubano called out to the Russian who headed for the wharf with four of his engineers. 'Nice work, we did it.'

'Don't celebrate yet,' Petrov said. 'Getting it in the water is the easy bit. Conducting all the trials we need in half the time required is the real challenge.'

'When will you do this static dive you talk about?' El Cubano asked. 'I'd like to have it underwater and out of sight.'

'We can only do it at the point when the tide is highest and there's around ten metres that will allow us to dive.'

'And when's that?'

'At 10pm if we manage to complete all the other trials in record time without a hitch.'

'It's amazing what you can do when you don't have an option,' El Cubano said. 'Don't worry, if you get her safely to the US, I'll give you a hundred thousand dollars bonus for your troubles.'

Petrov stared at him and then nodded, turning to his men. 'Let's go, we have a lot of work to do tonight.'

El Cubano's high security phone buzzed, the one he only shared with his top men in order to prevent it being wiretapped. He checked the caller. It was Hernando, who he had put in charge of coordinating the loading of the drugs from the shore to the barge and then to the submarine. 'What's up?'

'Boss, you'll never believe who we have here,' Hernando said.

CHAPTER THIRTY-EIGHT

When Luzma was dragged, blindfolded, to another room it was the stench she noticed first: stale urine, blood, and tobacco. Then she registered the muffled scream somewhere to her left. She lay on the cold cement floor and when she turned her head the pain was intense. She paused, trying not to black out again. The muffled scream continued. She eased herself up to sit, pulling her tattered dress over her chest. There were footsteps behind her and then the muffled cries intensified. She turned slowly towards the noise and pulled the blindfold off. She gasped and then began to cry, the sight of Jair brought her undone.

Jair's skinny body was tied to a chair in the corner. He was still wearing the same clothes he had on when she last saw him over two weeks ago, only now they were covered in blood and other stains. One eye was so badly bruised and swollen that it wouldn't open. The other was wide with fear and pain. She moved towards him, but before she could get far a boot lunged into her side, sending nauseating pain through her body. Jair's muffled screams increased and his chair screeched across the concrete as he squirmed wildly.

'Shut up, you whining little troublemaker.'

Just the sight of El Cubano and the sound of his voice filled her with fear and repulsion. She curled up and shuffled away from him. His face split into a smile.

'You thought you could get to me with that little video you and your boyfriend made, did you?'

More pain than before shot through her as he rammed his foot into her chest. She gasped for breath but there was no air.

'We found it in your bag. You are a brave little girl, aren't you?' He crouched down in front of her, grabbing her hair and pulling her face within an inch of his. His eyes were so dark they were almost black. 'Who have you shown it to?'

'No-one,' she said.

'Liar!' he said, dragging her across the room by her hair until she was before Jair.

She looked up at her brother, her vision blurred by the tears in her eyes. The very same feelings were reflected in his one open eye. She leaned her head onto his leg.

'Look up, bitch,' El Cubano shouted, snapping her head back towards him. He reached into the back of his jeans and pulled out a gun. He pointed it at Jair's head. Panic spiralled within Luzma.

'No, please don't,' she begged, crawling towards him and grabbing his legs. 'Take me instead. Please don't hurt him.'

El Cubano looked down at her, his eyes blank. She was on her knees now, stooping below him. The tattered top of her dress hung limply around her waist. She didn't care. She had to do something, anything, to stop him from killing Jair.

'Please take me instead,' she begged, looking up at him.

He glared at her and then back at Jair. Then he turned the gun on her, tracing it down the side of her face and over her exposed breast. Her skin crawled.

'You want your brother to watch, do you?' he whispered, crouching down before her and then he reached his other hand up her skirt. His fingers grabbed the corner of her underpants and twisted them around and then he began to pull.

Jair's muffled screams grew louder, the piercing sound of his chair scratching across the concrete.

Do something, Luzma. Don't let him do this to you, her mind screamed. But her body was frozen. All those years of self-defence training her father and then Uncle Jorge had given her seemed to be forgotten, suffocated by the terror she felt. Just like the last time.

El Cubano smiled sadistically as her cotton underpants ripped. His breathing was heavy.

'Just kill me,' she whispered and then repeated a little louder. 'Just kill me.'

The man stood over the top of her, the greenish light in the room shining off the top of his head and casting shadows in the creases that covered his face. The side of his mouth rose, revealing yellow teeth as he began to undo his belt. Luzma felt as cold and hard as the concrete floor she lay on.

El Cubano's belt jangled open and he undid his zipper. Repulsion seeped through her.

'You're not going to get away with this,' she said, but she felt powerless. Her fight had gone.

His laugh was sharp like a slap. 'Not going to get away with what exactly? If you're talking about this,' he said, pointing to his penis as he pulled down his underpants. 'Well, I can do whatever I want, to whoever I want, when I want. Little whores like you always give it up one way or another. When I see something I want, I take it and no-one ever gets in my way.'

The cold fear Luzma felt suddenly shifted to rage. She thought of all the other women he had raped, tortured and killed. She thought of the young girl whose tortured body was found hanging from a pole in San Francisco: another victim of the paramilitaries. She thought of the stories Diana told her. Then she thought of herself when she was only fifteen. Just a teenager whose innocence was lost in one moment. That paramilitary officer never had to pay either. Neither did those men who took her mum. These men never pay for their crimes so they are able to repeat them again and again with no consequence. The rage surged up from her gut. She clenched her fists, her nails digging into her hands. It wasn't fair that they could destroy so many lives without payback.

'If you're talking about that little video that you and your friend taped, you haven't achieved anything by giving it to the authorities. Only now, we'll make sure that you and your brother and the American have very long and painful deaths to make up for the inconvenience you've caused us.'

'They'll get you and you'll go to prison,' she said.

He bent down, pointing the gun at her chest and with his left hand pushed her legs apart. She fought back, squeezing them shut as hard as she could. Jair's cries grew more insistent. Her attacker pushed harder, his fingers digging into her thighs.

'What country are you living in?' he asked. 'We don't go to prison. We have friends in the right places who protect us, and let us know when little snitching whores like you give the authorities information. That way we can always outsmart the authorities.' He leaned forward, his right hand with the gun in it resting just beside Luzma's head and his face close to hers, his breath on her neck.

'They know what you're doing and they'll capture you.' Her voice trembled from a mixture of fear and rage.

He laughed and brought his face so close to hers that his sweat dropped onto her cheek. 'No, they knew what we were planning on doing and they thought they could track the submarine. But if you press the right buttons people will always do what you want and the electrician was no different. He cooperated very nicely.'

Luzma gasped. Mauricio, Diana's boyfriend. If he was killed it would be her fault.

'You see, your *gringo* friends think the submarine is still at the factory. That's what their little device is telling them, but by the time they go to the factory the submarine will be gone and the drugs will never have been there. Without the drugs or the submarine, they have nothing. And the tape isn't worth much without those who made it to back it up as evidence because all of those people will be dead.'

Luzma's face burned at the thought of El Cubano and the General walking away from everything they'd done without ever having to pay. Rage consumed her. Rage for everything that had been done to her and her family. Rage for all these innocent people across the country. Luzma turned away. His hand was resting to her left with the gun underneath it.

'Now fucking open your legs, you little whore, and give me some,' El Cubano said, his spit landing in her eye.

He moved his hand to get a better grip on her thighs and push her legs apart. It was the best chance she would get. She thought of all the years of training her father and Uncle Jorge had given her, of running through the pressure points that could debilitate a person. This time was different, this time she took a breath and let the rage inside her explode. She brought her right knee up as hard as she could into El Cubano's groin. At the same time she grabbed the gun, smashing it across his temple. He groaned and rolled to the side, disoriented. A heavy enough blow to the temple could knock someone out for several minutes her uncle had said. She scrambled to her feet and, drawing on all the fury she felt, smashed the side of the gun into his temple twice more.

She stood over him, the gun in her hand. She put her index finger on the trigger, the metal cold against her skin. She looked down at El Cubano, his pants halfway down his legs. He deserved to die and she could kill him so easily. The muffled screams returned. She looked at Jair.

'He deserves this,' she whispered. 'You heard him; men like him never face justice for their crimes. This is the only way to stop him.'

She stood over him and pointed the gun right at his forehead. She cocked it. Suddenly there was a loud bang at the door.

'Boss, you need to get moving if you're going to get to the pick-up point on time,' one of the men called out from the other room.

El Cubano stirred slightly.

If she shot him now his men would come straight in. She needed to save Jair. She slammed the side of the gun against his temple again to buy them more time. Then turned to Jair and tore off the ropes that tied his bloodied hands and feet to the chair and removed the gag. She motioned towards a second door at the back of the room.

El Cubano moaned again behind them. Adrenaline began to pump faster through Luzma's veins. They opened the door and stepped into a dark hallway, the dim light revealing another doorway at the end. Closing the door behind her, Luzma ran down the hall, holding the gun in one hand and pulling Jair along with her. She reached for the handle and turned. It moved a millimetre to the right and then jammed. She pulled harder, but it wouldn't budge.

Behind them El Cubano screamed, 'Get that fucking bitch!'

Luzma's heart pounded like a drum in her head. She was enshrouded in darkness apart from a tiny crack of light that seeped under the door. She still held the gun in her right hand and with her left she tried to feel around the door handle to locate the lock. Her hand was trembling so much that she couldn't steady it and it rattled the door handle. Jair bent down below her to feel around the bottom of the door. Suddenly there was a commotion in the room they had just left.

'What the fuck!' a man's voice in the other room rang out.

'Boys, get in here.'

'Don't worry about me,' El Cubano said. 'Just get her.'

There was a grating of metal against metal from where Jair was crouched. Luzma tried the handle again and this time it opened. The cold fresh air of the night hit her. She and Jair ran out into the narrow passageway at the back of the house and closed the door behind them. Just two metres to the right was the light of the street and to the left the darkness of a row of houses leading to the water. They ran to the corner, Luzma peered out around the building. At the other end of the house there were several men guarding the corner. There was no way they could go onto the road without the guards seeing them. She grabbed Jair's hand and ran back along the narrow pathway in the direction they had come. Past the door to the right was another passageway. They rounded the corner and began to run down it as fast as they could. Behind them the back door slammed open.

'Split up and find that bitch,' a man's voice shouted.

At the end of the passageway was a dimly lit street. Luzma pulled Jair around the corner. Behind them boots pounded against the ground. On the main road to their right, angry voices echoed through the night. She yanked Jair and they sprinted across the street to the darkness of the alleyway on the other side. They began to run down it and a dog in the house beside them barked. Jair's hand clawed into her as he tried to keep up.

'Faster!' she whispered.

'I c-c-can't. My l-l-leg.'

They didn't have time to deal with it so she continued to drag him behind her. The footsteps were not far behind. Luzma willed her legs and Jair's to move faster as they ran towards the next street. They reached it and skidded around the corner. A sharp pain bit into her foot as she stepped on broken glass. She gritted her teeth as they sped along the front of the house to the main road to the right. The sound of footsteps intensified behind them. As they reached the corner she didn't have to look around, she heard several of El Cubano's men running down the road towards them. They were trapped. The paramilitaries were coming to their left and right and if they ran forward they would be revealed by the streetlight. Luzma looked around wildly.

Jair yanked her hand. He was pulling her under the front of the stilted house. She followed him and they rolled beneath the house and then slid down to the water beneath. It was high tide and her body and head were totally submerged. The gun slipped through her fingers into the water. The coldness shocked her skin and she inhaled the water. She came to the surface, where there was less than half a metre to the bottom of the house. She tried not to cough up the water that was now in her lungs. She reached around for Jair but she grabbed onto something else, a large plastic bag filled with something hard. She suppressed a scream. Then she felt Jair's hand on her shoulder. Footsteps and voices were just above them. With Jair's hand holding on to her she began to swim to the left away from the voices.

'Where'd they go?' a man shouted.

'I don't know. I heard them running down here.'

'You check in front. You check down that way. You go left. You right and you below.'

The water was dark, with only small shards of light filtering in from the cracks in the floorboards above them. The men were now to their right as Luzma and Jair tried to slowly swim away without making any noise. The footsteps dispersed. But not all of them. Some continued to hover not far from them and then there was some noise and light to their right.

Luzma grabbed Jair and pulled him down with her under the water and behind a stilt of one of the homes. The light was nearly on top of them. Could El Cubano's men see them? The sound of her heartbeat was amplified under the water. The light continued to search for them. Luzma's lungs started to scream for air and Jair tugged at her hand, but she held him close to her. She began to feel lightheaded. Then there was darkness. She pushed to the surface and gulped in air, suppressing the desire to cough. She drew Jair close to her, his breath heavy and his body shivering.

Thank you, God.

CHAPTER THIRTY-NINE

L uzma had no idea what time it was. Her watch had stopped working at 1.05pm, its face now fogged with water. They had swum around the bay and then walked through the mangroves for what felt like hours on end in order to reach the centre of town. Her body hung heavily like the damp dress that covered her. Jair's arms were wrapped tightly around her waist; his head slumped against her shoulder. She held him tightly. She would never let him go again.

They hid in the shadows underneath the stilts of a bar, the mangroves and water behind them. The party from the music festival continued and the crowd was louder than a plague of locusts; chattering, shouting, car horns honking and, underneath it all, the thump of the drums. Above them the wooden boards groaned as feet thudded to the beat.

From where they were hidden they could just see the road, but between the commotion and Luzma's exhaustion it looked like a child's painting. She processed flashes of color and random inter-twined limbs. She rubbed her eyes, trying to focus. She thanked God that they had escaped and were alive, but they would not be safe until they were out of Buenaventura. She should get them out straightaway. But she couldn't just leave. She needed to stop El Cubano. She remembered him gloating about how he would get away with everything as he always did. She was determined that this time he and his cronies would not get away with the atrocities they had committed.

She needed to contact Nathaniel from the US Government, but her bag was gone and along with it the phone numbers she needed, money and Rafa's beloved camera. There was no-one they could trust. They couldn't get in a taxi or a bus because the likelihood of them working for the paramilitaries or the General was too high, not to mention the fact she no money. However, the longer she waited the better chance they would have of finding them. She closed her eyes, trying to block out the cacophony of noises around her. She tried to remember the phone number for the US agents, but she couldn't dredge anything up from the mire of her mind.

But one number bubbled to the surface. Rafa. Would he even answer? He had his phone turned off so he couldn't be traced. Maybe if he had escaped Buenaventura, as she hoped, he might be using it again.

She stood up straight, a new energy surging through her, like a second wind. She pulled Jair up and led him to the corner of the building. The noises grew louder. She surveyed the street. Just down the road was the entrance to the famous Dolphin Hotel, which had one of the best views in town from the rooftop, but they definitely wouldn't let her in looking like she did. Jair had given her his singlet, which was now ripping at the seams, and she had tied the broken straps of her dress around her neck, but still it hung limply off her body, brown with mud and rum and vomit. But she wasn't too out of place. After dancing all night, the people on the street were wet with sweat and their clothes were covered in dirt. To her left, half a block down the hill, there was a group of girls sitting on the sidewalk drinking beer and laughing. Maybe one of them would let her use their phone.

'Let's go find a phone,' she said, looking down at Jair. 'Your job is to keep a lookout for the paramilitaries or the General's men.'

The eye that was puffed and closed over twitched. He gripped tightly onto her hand.

'We're going to get out of here, I promise,' she said.

They wound their way through the crowd. Luzma kept her gaze trained on the ground. Bare feet danced beside black shoes and frayed and dusty skirt hems swooshed through the air. They arrived at the group of girls giggling at the side of the road. Luzma squatted before them.

'Excuse me. Do any of you have a phone? It's urgent.'

The laughter stopped. The group of girls stared at her, smiles fading and then they glanced at each other.

'Please, it's desperate.'

One girl reached down her top and pulled out a phone that was wedged between her breasts. The others laughed. She handed it to Luzma.

'Thank you so much. I won't be long.'

Luzma sat on the pavement, bent over, her spare hand cupping her ear as she dialed Rafa's number. *Please answer.*

'Hello.'

She let out her breath. Just hearing his voice was comforting.

'Rafa.'

'Luzma? Where are you? Are you okay? I've been worrying like crazy about you. I thought you were...'

'I'm in the centre on the main road up the hill in front of the Dolphin Hotel. I need to get out of here. I'm sure they're looking for us. I escaped with Jair. Where are you?' She was breathless.

'I'm here near the centre with Nathaniel and Jose from the DEA. We've been looking for you. We're coming straightaway, don't move.'

'How long will you be? I'm worried they might have men around the centre looking for us.' She peered to either side. Jair was pressed into her side.

'Five minutes, ten absolute maximum. Where are you exactly?'

'We're sitting on the sidewalk on the other side of the road in front of the hotel.'

'We're leaving now. Do not leave that area no matter what.'

As soon as Luzma saw Rafa, her body relaxed. The nightmare was nearly over, surely. He stood in the middle of the crowd, looking around until he found her. She leapt to her feet, bringing Jair with her. Rafa pushed towards her and she buried herself in his chest. His strong arms wrapped around them both.

'Thank God you're safe,' he said. 'We've got to get you out of here. Nathaniel is waiting with the car just around the corner.'

Luzma noticed Jose Guevara. He stood beside them, his eyes monitoring the area. She held onto Jair tightly as they wound through the crowd. There were flashes of color and movement all around them but all she felt was the warmth of the two bodies on either side of her.

A block away a large black SUV was pulled over to the side of the road with the motor running. Inside Nathaniel turned, looking at Jair and Luzma, his forehead furrowed. He hit the central lock after they were all in.

'What happened?'

She opened her mouth, but her jaw felt stiff. She didn't know where to start.

'They had us.' Like a blocked tap that is finally released words fell out of her mouth in staccato bursts. 'El Cubano was about to kill us, but we got away. You need to arrest him. You need to stop them. They have Mauricio. They will kill him if he isn't already dead. You need to save him. The submarine has left.'

'Whoa, slow down,' Nathaniel said, his hands up. 'They have Mauricio?'

'Yes, El Cubano said that they knew what he was up to and forced him to cooperate with them. They're going to kill him. You have to stop them. He's in this situation because he's helping you.' She leaned forward and grabbed Nathaniel's arm. 'Please, you have to help him.'

Nathaniel's body seemed to contract. His brow creased heavily. It was the first time Luzma had seen such strong emotion on his face.

'Tell us exactly what El Cubano said to you.'

'The submarine has left. They've tricked you.'

Before she could say any more Jose interrupted. 'What do you mean it has left? The signal hasn't changed. It has to still be in the factory.'

Nathaniel shook his head, his hand gripping his thigh. 'If they've tortured Mauricio, they know about the tracking device. What else did they say?'

'He said he would get away with everything because you think the submarine is still in the factory. But I know where they've taken it. We need to go there now.'

'He told you where they were going to take it?' Nathaniel asked, his voice incredulous.

Luzma shuddered. She didn't want to think about what had happened. She pushed her dress down between her legs. She tried to clear the image of the men surrounding her from her mind. She needed to focus on stopping El Cubano.

'They called El Cubano to let him know they had me. One of his men talked about a 4.30 transfer. I know the place they mentioned; we passed it on our way to Buenaventura from my hometown. We need to get there to stop them.'

'Tell us where it is and we can do something about it,' Nathaniel said.

'I'm coming with you.'

'Luzma,' Rafa interjected.

'We're not taking a civilian on a military operation,' Nathaniel said. 'If you want to help, tell us what you know.'

She had to go. The only way this nightmare would be truly over was when she saw El Cubano and the General either arrested or dead. She wouldn't let them get away with what they had done.

'I have the information and I know where the place is. But if you want my help you need to promise that you're taking me with you.'

'Fine. Hurry up,' Nathaniel said.

'They talked about a pick up at Bezan,' she said.

'How far is it?' Nathaniel asked.

'It took us several hours from there to the main wharf in Buena-ventura. But we were travelling on a small motorised canoe. There's also road access. We got off while they were refuelling. At the end of the wharf there's a small general store and a dirt road.'

Nathaniel shook his head as he looked at his watch. 'It's 2.15. We have two hours and fifteen minutes. I have to call Chuck immediately.'

CHAPTER FORTY

'Has there been any movement or change whatsoever in the tracking device?' Chuck asked the CIA duty officer over the phone.

There was a long pause. Chuck checked his watch. There was just over two hours before the scheduled pick up Nat had told him about. Surely it would be impossible to pull off the operation in such a short timeframe. Even before considering that, he needed to check that the information was credible.

Chuck stood at the window. The mountains that loomed behind the apartment were a dark mass against the charcoal sky, apart from a large illuminated marble statue of Jesus supposedly looking after his people.

'I'm just checking through the logs. There was a small change at around 6pm last night. But it was minimal and after that there was no further change so it wasn't considered to be outside normal operational movements,' the agent reported.

'Is it possible that the device could have been removed and placed somewhere else?'

'It's not impossible, but, that seems unlikely. The device would be hard to locate as it's wired into the power system and it would be very difficult to move it with minimal detection. These are drug smugglers not rocket scientists, surely they would have destroyed it immediately and we would know.'

Chuck considered the man's words. He was right, of course. But he didn't know the full story. They had the electrician and had presumably tortured him until he had led them to the device. He had been trained by Nat on how to handle the device, place it and move it if needed. They must also have electronic engineers if the submarine included the kind of technology that their intel had reported.

'Is there anything else, sir?' the CIA agent asked, breaking through Chuck's thoughts.

'No, that's all.' Chuck took a deep breath and called Martin Savoy, the US Military Attaché based in the US Embassy. He was following the submarine operation closely and was their only chance of getting fast approval from the Pentagon and the Colombians.

'Hello,' Martin Savoy answered calmly.

'It's Chuck. We have an emergency. I need you to get approval from the Pentagon for an immediate action.'

'What's happened?'

Chuck explained. With every minute that passed, their chances of finding the submarine faded.

'If we lose the submarine now, we have little chance of finding it again. We have to intercept while they're loading the drugs at Bezan.'

'Which you say is happening in just over ninety minutes.' Scepticism dripped from Martin's voice.

It was the same way Chuck felt, but they had to give it a shot.

'If we can get Pentagon approval at least we can get a satellite image of the area to start with so we can monitor what's going on.'

'What about the Colombian Attorney-General? How the hell do you think we're going to get him onboard within an hour and a half in the middle of the night?' Martin was always a straight shooter, but this morning he was particularly blunt.

'We'll have to bring the Colombians onboard. They can seize the drugs and make arrests and we can just act as backup. The Buenaventura Special Navy Unit could be our best bet,' Chuck said, 'but the DEA needs to keep a low profile. I'll send Nat and Jose and that's it. The request should come from you, saying it's intel we've just received. We don't want them to know we've been tracking this for two months and haven't brought them into the picture.'

Chuck had purposely left the Colombian authorities out of the operation. He had worked with many good men and women whom he highly respected. But drug money had infected every part of this society and he knew plenty of officials who had been on the cartels' books. He'd coordinated operations with the Colombian Elite Police Force who were in charge of the drug hunt many times, but for an operation as important and sensitive as this, he'd only wanted to inform those who absolutely needed to know in order to minimize the risk of it being leaked.

'So what exactly do we need from the Pentagon?'

'Satellite with thermal imaging of the area. It looks pretty isolated, so at 4.30am the only movement should be coming from our target. If we can get a boat there in time as backup for the Buenaventura Special Navy Unit, that would be good.'

'And you want all of this launched in the next hour?' Martin sounded doubtful.

'Look, Martin, we're talking about the first ever submarine of this calibre that we're aware of. We know it has the capability to hold up to ten tons of cocaine. We can't afford to let that be released in the US market. I understand that what I'm asking for is near impossible, but we've got to do it.'

Martin sighed. 'I'll call Southcom to get permission for the operation and once I have that I'll get you the satellite images of the area. I'll try to find a boat close enough to get there in time and we'll approach the Buenaventura Special Navy Unit to mobilize a small team immediately.'

'Thank you, Martin,' Chuck said, pulling on his clothes as he spoke. 'I'll get a team together with some of our leads in Virginia and will see you at the Embassy when you can get there.'

'Will do,' Martin said and hung up.

Chuck looked at the clock. 2.40am. Martin was right, it would be close to impossible to pull off such an operation.

CHAPTER FORTY-ONE

'We need to leave now,' Luzma said, staring impatiently at the two agents in the front of the vehicle. She needed to get them moving. 'You can't let El Cubano get away.'

They were parked in front of the entrance to the Buenaventura naval base. Two officers stood at the gate gripping their assault rifles. Echoes from the ongoing party in the centre of town played across the water but the street where they were parked was quiet.

'What do you think we're doing, having a coffee break?' Nathaniel stared at her in the rear-view mirror. 'If it was me making the final decisions we'd be there now.'

Luzma glanced at Jair, who sat beside her, with Rafa on the other side. Just looking at his bruised and swollen face made her all the more determined not to let El Cubano get away with this.

'What are you going to do about Mauricio?'

'I've asked for a team to be ready to go to San Francisco to search the factory and other areas for him,' Nathaniel said. He paused, his face showed pain. 'But we need to be realistic; the chances of him still being alive are slim.'

The thought made Luzma feel sick with guilt.

The phone on the dashboard rang. Nathaniel grabbed it. 'Chuck, please tell me you've got good news for me.'

'Excellent. We're going to stop these bastards,' he said into the phone. 'Do you have an image of the target?'

He paused and then continued. 'How close do you want us for now?'

Nathaniel hung up and grabbed a handgun from the glove box. 'The Special Navy Unit is in. Let's go,' he said to Jose.

Luzma jumped out of the car, motioning for Jair and Rafa to follow her.

The two guards at the front of entrance stepped forward and one spoke into his radio.

'Get back in the car. There's no way you can all come with us, it's too dangerous,' Nathaniel said, handing Luzma the car keys.

She stared at him. What was he thinking?

'We made a deal,' she said, fiercely. 'I told you all the information I heard and in return, you take me with you. And you can't just leave Jair and Rafa in the car. It's not safe.'

Nathaniel hesitated and then motioned them forward. 'Fine, you can come. But the others need to stay inside the Navy base where it is safe.'

Luzma, Nathaniel and Jose made their way briskly towards the jetty where there was an array of naval vessels, from patrol boats to frigates. The engines of two patrol boats revved to life and a small team of navy Special Forces officers moved about the decks.

A stocky muscular man wearing full naval battle gear with a bulletproof vest and helmet and a M-16 slung over his shoulder approached them.

'I'm Commander Romero.' He shook their hands, his grip firm as if asserting his position. He pointed to the two vessels beside them. 'We have two boats for tonight's mission, *La Tigre*, which is a new aluminium 35-footer that was given to us by your government to help in the fight against drugs and the *Bravado 2*, an older model, steel hulled 50-footer. Both vessels are armed with Browning M2 .50 calibre on the foredeck. I'll be aboard the *Bravado 2* and you'll be with Lieutenant Gonzalez on *La Tigre*.'

'We need the road access covered as well in case some of El Cubano's men try to escape that way,' Nathaniel said. 'They need to be stationed close to the wharf.'

'We have a vehicle with four men about to leave. Lieutenant Cuevas will lead them. We shouldn't need more as the action is going to be in the water.'

Nathaniel turned to Luzma, who stood beside him. 'You go in the vehicle. It should be safer.'

'I'm not interested in safety. I want to see him caught,' she said, defiant.

———

Chuck arrived at the US Embassy and made his way to the lift that would take him to the operations room below ground known as the 'Dungeon'. He entered his pass into the code reader and the lift door opened. He then took the stairs two at a time down to another security door, this time entering a separate code into a keypad. The doors slid open to reveal the operations room with an 80-inch screen along the rear wall and the latest video conferencing equipment. His second in command, Sean Perry, along with Martin Savoy and the CIA and DEA night-time duty officers sat at the long table. Ronald Smith, the DEA International Coordinator of the operations against the Norte de Valle Cartel, was on one of the screens, dark circles under his eyes highlighting the lack of sleep they had all had.

'Thank you all for being here at this hour and on such short notice,' Chuck said, taking a seat and then turning to Martin. 'What's the update with the CIA satellite image now that we have approval?'

'I put in the request as top priority so we should have it any time now. You owe me big time for pulling this off for you,' he said.

'I know and I'm damned impressed.'

The main screen flickered to life and a woman appeared. 'Good morning, I'm Duty Officer Susan Simpson. I have ST15 with thermal imaging capabilities focused on the small township of Bezan at 77 degrees, 11 minutes west and 3 degrees, 50 minutes north as requested.'

The woman's face narrowed to a small frame in the top right-hand corner as the satellite image took up the screen. The image was dark with the faint outline of the shore, wharves and a number of small boats visible. A small cluster of red dots took up the upper left hand corner of the screen.

'Morning, Susan.' Chuck nodded at the woman. 'What's the cluster of red dots that the heat sensors are picking up in the top left?'

'By the size of them it appears to be a herd of cattle. Apart from that, there's not a lot of activity.'

Chuck glanced at Martin, swallowing hard. What if the intelligence was incorrect? Or even worse, what if this was a distraction and the real operation was going on as planned. How would he explain that to the Pentagon and the CIA?

'Is this definitely Bezan that we're looking at?' he asked.

The woman's forced a curt smile. 'Yes, sir, this is the foreshore of the township of Bezan as requested.'

'Can you scan out to see if there's anything of interest in the area?'

The camera immediately zoomed out one thousand metres showing nothing but the darkness of the water.

'What's that in the top right?' Chuck stood up and walked closer to the screen.

'That's about five hundred meters offshore. Let me center in on it and zoom to one hundred metres.'

As the image narrowed, a grey outline of a rectangular vessel became clear. The infrared camera revealed a few red dots around the sides of the vessel.

'It's definitely not a submarine, it's too large. It looks more like a barge,' Sean said. 'It's probably one of the timber barges that frequent this channel.'

'Pull back out, Susan,' Chuck said. The problem was they didn't know if the drugs were coming by water or land. He was sure the cartel had numerous jungle laboratories in the area that they had yet to discover. And the tributary system that wound throughout the Pacific coast made it a perfect place for the cartels to move the drugs undetected.

'What's that?' he asked, pointing to a small object that appeared in the middle left-hand side of the screen that was moving towards Bezan.

The satellite image zoomed in revealing what seemed to be a speedboat with half a dozen red dots onboard.

'It's not our submarine but I bet it belongs to the cartel,' Chuck said. 'Pull back out and keep the vessel in focus.'

As Susan pulled back on the image another similar sized vessel appeared in the right-hand lower corner of the image. Both were heading towards Bezan.

'Party time,' Chuck said.

The first speedboat arrived at the wharf in Bezan, while the other moved closer. Then, as if from nowhere, another grey shape appeared at the end of the wharf.

'Susan, zoom in on that,' Chuck said. 'Sean, get Nat on the phone.'

The tube-shaped image at the end of the wharf became clearer and small red dots appeared across it

'We need them to intercept now.'

'Move it!' El Cubano bellowed. 'I want the submarine under water in ten minutes.'

He stood on the deck of his speedboat that had just pulled up at the wharf. The submarine was tied to the end and the other speedboat, carrying the drugs, was tied to the other side of the wharf.

El Cubano's head throbbed with pain, but he didn't have time to think about it. He had bigger things to worry about. That fucking bitch could have told the authorities by now that the tracking device had been moved and they would send out a search party. He needed the submarine underwater before they could find them. A raw fury curdled inside of him just thinking about her. He gnashed his teeth as he thought how he would make her pay. Now, he needed the drugs and the submarine out of here. That way they would have no proof against him. He needed to keep his focus.

His men scuttled between the speedboat and the submarine carrying blocks of top-grade cocaine, each 30 kilograms in weight. The Russian captain and the head Russian engineer stood at the top of the conning tower supervising the loading. They kept light to a minimum, just two small spotlights so as not to draw attention as El Cubano had ordered. But they were moving too slowly.

'Faster!' El Cubano shouted. 'I want this finished in less than five minutes.'

They'd loaded less than a quarter of the cocaine when El Cubano heard a noise. He stiffened. 'Can you hear that?'

Everyone was quiet, frozen in position. The distant sound of engines became clearer.

'*Puta mierda.*' His body shook with rage. He turned to his men and the Russian skipper. 'Get as much cocaine as you can onboard immediately and get out of here. I'll radio you later with an alternate pick up.'

'Don't worry,' the skipper responded, 'they won't catch me.'

El Cubano hoped he was right. He was a dead man if the submarine was caught. He turned to his men who were desperately loading blocks of cocaine onto the submarine. 'We must give the submarine a chance to escape. When they get too close open fire from both of the speedboats.'

The men stared at him mutely. Normally they would be ordered to sink the small boat they were on, taking the cocaine – and thus the evidence – down with it. But he couldn't let them capture the submarine, no matter how outgunned they were likely to be.

'Chuck, we're one hundred and fifty metres away,' Nathaniel shouted over the top of the roaring engine. 'Confirm the target is still in position.'

He stood on the fly bridge beside the young captain as they hurtled forward, flying across the surface, hitting waves with a jarring thud. They rode in darkness, trying not to get far ahead of the *Bravado 2*. The only light came from the moon reflecting across the water. Surely they had them now with the two navy vessels surrounding them and the four officers blocking the road exit at the end of the wharf.

'Confirmed,' came the reply.

'We've spotted the target,' Commander Romero said over the radio. 'We're about to light them up.'

The *Bravado 2* was now alongside *La Tigre* and only seventy metres from the target.

Two powerful spotlights revealed the submarine tied to the end of wharf, flanked by two speedboats at either side.

'We've got them!' Nathaniel exclaimed, hitting his fist on the seat. He turned to Jose who stood behind him. 'Check out the size of the submarine. They weren't messing around.'

'This is the Colombian Navy,' the commander's voice bellowed over the speaker of the *Bravado 2*. 'Drop your weapons and prepare to be boarded.'

A shower of bullets slammed into the super structure of *La Tigre* and *Bravado 2*. Nathaniel and the rest of the crew dived to the deck, trying to find cover wherever they could. It sounded like a hailstorm as the bullets smacked into the aluminium vessels and bulletproof glass.

'What the hell!' Nat exclaimed, looking around to make sure no-one was hit.

The navy officers were already crawling into position, M-16 automatic rifles ready. They returned fire.

'Bear away and regroup at a hundred metres,' Romero's voice boomed across the radio. 'Let's see how the stupid bastards feel about the M2 cannon.'

One of the Special Forces crawled onto the deck of *Bravado 2* into the steel screen protection around the Browning M2 cannon. Nat grabbed the radio.

'*Bravado 2* come in. We need El Cubano alive. Restrict fire. Repeat, restrict fire.' But his voice couldn't be heard over the top of the deafening thunder of the Browning M2.

Nat snatched the night glasses to get a better look at the submarine. The two speedboats were riddled with holes and several of the paramilitaries were down. He couldn't see El Cubano. As he watched, one of the submarine crew released the bowlines and was running the gauntlet across the deck towards the conning tower when a bullet slammed into the man's chest. An older man with a grey beard released the stern line and dashed for the conning tower. He quickly scrambled up the ladder and disappeared below.

'Fuck, the submarine's about to dive!' Nat yelled, as the submarine began to float away from the barge.

'A group of them are escaping down the wharf!' Luzma said. She and Lieutenant Cuevas and his three navy officers in the car were staring at the wharf about 200 metres in front of them. A constant chatter of machine-gun fire rattled the air. At the end of the wharf sparks of orange flew in every direction.

Dawn was nearing and in the soft early morning light Luzma could make out five figures moving down the wharf. She felt sure that one of them would be El Cubano. He was a coward and would happily leave his men to fight while he fled to safety. Her body tensed again at the thought of him. She should have killed him when she had the chance before he could hurt anyone else.

'We need to cut them off when they reach the main road through town,' she said, pointing to the dirt road that led past the end of the wharf.

'If they hit the jungle or the mangroves that surround the area it will be harder to catch them.'

'Wait until they're at the end of the wharf and then take them by surprise in the vehicle,' said Lieutenant Cuevas who sat in the front passenger seat. Turning to the two officers that sat either side of Luzma. 'Get ready to get out and pursue them on foot and make sure the girl stays down and out of the way.'

'You're outnumbered. Let me help you. I know how to shoot a gun,' she said. She was prepared to do anything to stop El Cubano.

'This is a military operation and it's not safe for a civilian. You must stay inside the vehicle.'

'I can handle myself,' Luzma said.

The man cut her off. 'You stay in the car.'

Luzma consented, deciding it was easier to do as he said. She watched as the man beside her prepared himself. He pulled back the T-bar at the top of his rifle, slid the small lever on the right side back and checked the pouch of magazines attached to his waist. He unclipped the pistol that was attached to the other side of his belt. He pulled the chamber back to check ammunition and then, with his right thumb, pulled the lever down and back into firing mode. She thought of her father and uncle taking her through similar motions.

'Ready?' the leader asked.

'Yes, sir.' The men responded.

The vehicle revved to life then sped forward.

'Get ready to jump out. They're heading for the jungle.'

Luzma was thrown from one side to the other as the vehicle sped along the dirt track. Her head rammed into the side of the front seat as the vehicle slammed to a halt.

'Go!'

The officers jumped out of the car. Suddenly gunfire exploded through the air. The officer to Luzma's right used the door as a partial shield as he peered around the corner of it. The man to her left had already moved forward. She looked around the vehicle, wondering if there was anything she could use as a weapon.

'Colombian Navy,' Lieutenant Cuevas's voice called out. 'Drop your weapons.'

The paramilitaries responded by spraying the car with bullets. Luzma crouched down. The officer to her left fell back against the open door and slid to the ground.

Luzma moved to the open door, hunched over. Below her the man was doubled over, blood pumping out of his left temple. There was no use trying to help him.

The gunfire was moving further away, in the direction of the front of the car. From her position Luzma could make out a lone figure moving through the jungle in the opposite direction of the gunfire. He was headed back past the car towards the road they had come in on. As he stepped out from behind a bush only fifty metres away Luzma recognised El Cubano. She looked around the car. Three men lay on the ground nearby: two paramilitaries and another navy officer. The remaining two navy officers were at least fifty metres in front of the car, moving away from her, following the remaining paramilitaries.

Had they not seen El Cubano? Were they going to let him escape? She had to stop him. She jumped out of the car, staring at the dead officer in front of her. The automatic rifle lay on the ground beside him. She decided she would be better to take his pistol, as it was more familiar to her from all the training she had received from her father and uncle. She looked up. El Cubano was moving rapidly. She would not let him get away this time.

—

'Ram it!' Nathaniel ordered.

The young skipper's eyes widened. 'Ram it?'

'We can't let the sub escape. It is about to dive.' Nat's hulk-like frame loomed over the young man. 'Come around hard to the right and ram just in front of the conning tower. It's the only way to stop it.'

'I can't do that, sir.'

Nat looked wildly from the submarine to the skipper. The sub began to submerge. He grabbed the man's shoulders. 'If you don't ram it, we'll lose it. Do it!'

The skipper shook his head. Nat couldn't let the sub escape. He shoved the skipper to the side and grabbed the wheel, spinning it to turn the boat hard to the right towards the submarine's bow that was now just below the water with only the conning tower visible. He pushed forward on the twin throttles and *El Tigre* surged ahead. He needed to ram in front of the conning tower to have any hope of stopping the sub. Bullets flew past the open back of the boat. *El Tigre* was at full speed as it approached the submarine, which was rapidly disappearing underwater.

'Stop!' the skipper screamed.

Nathaniel couldn't stop. He had to capture the submarine.

'Hold on!' Nathaniel yelled.

They weren't going to make it. The conning tower passed in the front of their bow as they rammed the submerging submarine. *El Tigre's* bow came clear of the water with the screech of metals colliding. They made contact just aft of the conning tower and the sub continued to move forward and down with a grating sound that shuddered through *El Tigre*. Then it was gone. Jose and the skipper were catapulted into the front of the pilothouse. Nathaniel was flung sidewards, his head smashing against the side of the boat as he fell to the ground.

Nat's left temple pounded. He jumped to his feet and leaned over the side of the boat, his eyes darting wildly. *El Tigre* was still upright in the water, but the submarine was gone, leaving only ripples. A bullet thudded against the pilothouse less than a metre from Nathaniel's head. He pulled back, looking around dazed.

'You thought you were going to get away with it, didn't you?' Luzma said.

El Cubano stopped and turned to face her. She was about thirty meters behind him. She had followed him to the edge of the road without him noticing.

'You!' He walked towards her.

Luzma braced herself pointing the pistol at his chest.

213

'You wrecked our whole operation! I'm going to finish what I started with you!'

'You kidnapped and tortured my brother! You abused me!' Her voice was so hard it was unrecognizable. 'How many people have you killed, tortured and raped?'

'You liked it. You came back for more.'

Her finger started to put pressure on the trigger.

'No. I came back to stop you.'

'You wouldn't shoot me.'

'Really?' She wanted him dead.

He took a few steps closer. Now he was only fifteen metres away.

'What have you done with Mauricio?'

'Who?'

'Mauricio, the electrician who worked for you.'

'The traitor?' he scoffed. 'He's dead like you will be.'

El Cubano reached to the back of his pants and started to pull out a handgun. Luzma squeezed the trigger, hitting him in the shoulder. El Cubano spun around, stumbling backwards, falling to the ground, and dropping his gun.

Luzma walked over to him and picked up his gun.

'You bitch,' El Cubano held his right shoulder, his face contorted in pain. He moaned, doubling over as a crimson stain spread across his shirt. She pointed the gun at his chest, but her hand shook. She had never killed anyone before.

'You're going to pay,' he said, struggling to sit up.

She wanted to finish it. He deserved to die after all that he had done. In one simple movement she could kill him. Buenaventura would be a safer place without him. Her finger was pressed against the trigger, ready.

'Do it,' he said, his voice weakening.

She tried to slow her breathing to stop the shaking.

'You women are pathetic. You don't have the courage to kill me.'

Luzma held back her rage. What would she achieve killing him? One of his men would step in and continue to do exactly as El

Cubano had. Killing him at close range would make her just like him. She exhaled slowly. He needed to be brought to justice to make a real difference, not killed like this.

'Killing someone takes no courage. It's what spineless cowards like you do,' Luzma said calmly.

CHAPTER FORTY-TWO

'Will he come after us again?' Jair asked, looking up at Luzma. His eye was still so badly swollen he could only partially open it.

Luzma's throat tightened. She still couldn't believe she had almost lost her beloved brother. They sat at the end of the jetty. The calm water in front of them a contrast to the buzz of activity behind them as navy officers hauled large containers from their speedboats to the naval base. If those containers were full of cocaine, as Luzma assumed they must be, then they had seized a lot of it.

She pulled Jair closer. She didn't want to let him go again. 'You're safe now.'

'Promise?'

Luzma glanced at Rafa who sat beside them. He smiled awkwardly. He was probably thinking the same; how could anyone ever be totally safe in Colombia when the country was so infested with people like El Cubano and the General?

She didn't want to lie to Jair so she changed the subject.

'Doesn't he remind you of Grandpa?' She pointed to an old man in an artisanal canoe laden with fish rowing past. 'We'll be with them tomorrow.'

Nathaniel walked down the jetty towards them. 'Thank you for all you've done. El Cubano is in custody where he belongs. It wouldn't have happened without you.'

'Have you found the submarine?' Luzma asked.

He looked out at the bay, the disappointment clear. 'Not yet. But we will. We have several US and Colombian vessels monitoring the area. It has to surface sooner or later. We'll be there when it does.'

'And Mauricio?'

'We haven't found his body yet,' he said, looking at the ground.

'Well, back to it. Thank you again.'

Nathaniel turned quickly before Luzma could reply and walked away.

Jair looked up at Luzma. 'What will happen to El Cubano?'

'He'll live,' she said, recalling him being taken away, his shirt covered in blood. He had been conscious but silent for once.

'Do you think he'll go to jail where he can't hurt anyone else?' Jair asked.

Luzma looked down at her brother's bruised face. Colombia was full of people like El Cubano and General Ordonez who were free to do what they wanted. Maybe that could change. She was certainly willing to do whatever it took to stop people like them from hurting anyone else.

'He and others like him will go to jail because we will make sure of it.'

AUTHOR'S NOTE

While the story and characters in *A Reluctant Warrior* are fictitious, they are informed by events I witnessed and researched during the years I worked in human rights in Colombia and later in Washington DC as the Director of the U.S. Office on Colombia.

During this time, I interviewed thousands of victims of paramilitaries, guerrilla and drug cartels and met with senior leaders of these groups to understand exactly how they operate. I know Buenaventura intimately, including the most notorious neighborhoods featured in the book.

I wrote *A Reluctant Warrior* to help shine a light on the way ordinary Colombian citizens have suffered and continue to suffer, despite the advancement in the Peace Agreement. But more than that, I wrote it to celebrate, support and amplify the message of the brave people who risk their lives to protect and make a difference to others.

I have been blessed to work alongside incredibly inspiring human rights defenders within Colombia and throughout the world, who all work towards a better Colombia. I remember one day in Washington, D.C. when I was accompanying some of my Colombian human rights colleagues to testify at a Congressional hearing we'd organised. I was so nervous at the thought of it. I asked one of my colleagues if he felt the same. He said he felt more nervous about going home and the ramifications of speaking out so publicly. Indeed, he had received numerous death threats and attempts on his life because of the work he did and doing so in such a high-level forum would just amplify the risk. But that didn't stop him. Nor has it stopped the hundreds of incredible human rights defenders across Colombia that I've had the privilege to work with. They risk their life on an ongoing basis to fight for a more peaceful and just Colombia where all people are respected and protected. Their courage, tenacity and passion inspire me.

I am sure this book would never have been written if it weren't for the continued support of my parents. Thank you, Dad, for all your help developing and researching the submarine element of the narrative, and for helping ensure the technical accuracy; the story wouldn't be what it is today without that help. 'Thank you' must go to my mum for being my first ever editor. I am forever grateful for both of you for your encouragement and belief in me over the eight years it took to research, write and publish this book.

I also owe a huge thanks to retired Special Agent and former agent in charge of the U.S. Drug Enforcement Administration (DEA) Bogota country office, Joe AToft. We've never actually met, yet over a more than two-year period you diligently replied to my seemingly never-ending questions and even revised the book for me to ensure it's accuracy from a drug enforcement perspective. Thank you also to Jerry Salameh, Joe's DEA colleague, for helping a very techni-cally challenged person (me) understand how one would hide a tracking device on a submarine and operate it. And thanks must also go to Captain John Dikkenberg for all your help in researching the submarine and ensuring the technical accuracy.

I am particularly thankful to have found my publisher, Lou Johnson of The Author People. What I love about working with you is how you really care about the story behind the story, my passion for writing this novel and the difference it could make. Thanks should also go to my husband for convincing me to contact Lou in the first place!! Thanks also to the editorial team from The Manuscript Agency, particularly Jody Lee. And 'cheers' to David Compton for his earlier edits.

Finally, thanks to my friends and colleagues who have read the book and provided feedback and encouragement, especially Diana for all your help.

Kelly Brooke Nicholls xxx

THE FACTS
BEHIND THE STORY

If you'd like to learn more about the real-life stories that inspired this novel, visit Kelly's website www.kellybrookenicholls.com for interviews, videos, in-depth information. You can also discover more about the incredible Afro-Colombian culture.

For now here are some quick facts behind the story[1]:
- There have been 7.9 million victims of the armed conflict; almost half of them are women.
- Sexual violence, mostly used as a tool of war, has been widespread with 6.9 million people forcefully displaced from their homes and communities.
- 267,000 people have been killed in the conflict, many of them innocent civilians.
- The Office of the Attorney General has recorded 4,392 victims of possible extrajudicial executions.
- There have been 46,386 victims of forced disappearance.
- 29,622 kidnappings.
- 8,022 child soldiers used by paramilitaries and guerrilla groups.
- Around 300 million people around the world have reportedly consumed cocaine in their lifetime. Approximately half of this cocaine comes from Colombia[2].
- Colombian drug lords have been using 'narco-submarines', a type of custom-made ocean-going self-propelled submersible vessel, since at least 1993. They were used to export cocaine from Colombia to Mexico and built in the jungle.
- Since 2000 several true submarines being built or used by drug traffickers have been discovered[3].

[1] Amnesty International, 'Human Rights in Colombia in 10 Numbers', *7 October 2016* www.amnesty.org/en/latest/news/2016/10/human-rights-in-colombia

[2] Adriaan Alsema, Colombia Reports, 'Drug Trafficking in Colombia' colombiareports.com/drug-trafficking-in-colombia

[3] *Wikipedia*, 'Narco Submarines' en.wikipedia.org/wiki/Narco-submarine

Kelly Brooke Nicholls

Kelly Brooke Nicholls' fascination with other cultures was instilled in her early years growing up on a boat in the south pacific islands. She's been passionate about human rights from an early age and has over 15 years' senior leadership experience working for NGOs including an extended period living and working in Colombia.

Her extensive time living and working in Colombia has left an indelible mark. She has travelled extensively to places few foreigners have been, researching and documenting the impact of the ongoing war on ordinary citizens and the horrendous human rights abuses inflicted on them.

Kelly strongly believes that everyone has the ability to make a difference in the world and bring about positive change, and has spent her life helping people achieve that.

Kelly lives on the Northern Beaches of Sydney with her Colombian husband and two sons.

Keep up to date with Kelly at
www.kellybrookenicholls.com
and
http://www.theauthorpeople.com/kellybrooke-nicholls

CPSIA information can be obtained
at www.ICGtesting.com
Printed in the USA
BVOW03s1514190617
487257BV00001B/18/P